JUSTICE SERVED

R.G. Crossley

3RD STREET PUBLISHING

Dedication

For Rita with all my love, always.

Table of Contents

Introduction

I sit here in my office writing this introduction wondering how this marvellous journey started. The truth is my writing life started more than ten years ago when I first met Kristine Katherine Rusch and Dean Wesley Smith two professional writers who became my teachers and my mentors. Seven years ago I made my first professional sale which has been repeated many times after that first sale. A first sale is a wonderful experience and something you will never forget no matter how many sales you make.

It has been quite a journey and I thought this collection would represent my journey as a writer.

In this collection you will find stories about police detectives and criminals, serial killers, and victims of crime, odd characters, failed writers, and a detective with a conscience. This is a diverse collection which I hope you will enjoy. If you find these stories entertaining keep an eye out for more of my stories since I love to share them with you.

If you want to contact me, look for me on Facebook and Twitter, or through one of my websites. I'd love to hear from you.

Justice Served

R.G. CROSSLEY

**Published by 53rd Street Publishing
www.53rdstreetpublising.com**

Logo image by:

Engraver | Dreamstime.com

ISBN 978-1-927621-00-4

This is a work of fiction.

All characters, organization and events depicted
are products of the author's imagination.

Drip!

THE GREEN GLOW from the cheap radio alarm clock said it started at two a.m. precisely. A deafening drip forced Will Aston's red-rimmed eyes open and his rail-thin, pasty body to bolt upright on the lumpy, uncomfortable mattress.

Somewhere a dripping tap had interrupted his already tenuous attempt at slumber.

It had taken him five hours and five hundred miles to find this isolated motel off route seventy-three. He was desperate to find peace and quiet and sleep.

Now the drip had ruined everything.

First there was one, then two, then more in an ever-increasing crescendo. It began to sound like a steel drummer was playing inside his head.

Drip

Will hung his head in his hands, his naked body coated in a sheen of stale sweat.

The thin white bed sheet clung to him like plastic kitchen wrap.

It's hot. Too hot.

The temperature outside was nearly ninety. The dust covered air conditioner stuck in the window of the ancient motel room didn't work. It was likely much hotter in the room.

The wizened motel manager, a man with a fringe of gray round his bald head, who looked to be as old as the outside temperature, told him the reason the air conditioner didn't work was due to the rolling black outs that frequently plagued this part of the country. Of course, Will didn't believe him.

The ancient springs in the mattress squealed in protest as he lowered his bare feet to the thin maroon carpet beside the bed.

They probably heard me in the next county.

He padded into the tiny kitchen to check the kitchen sink tap first. He ran a finger round the spigot and found it was dry. He next checked the bathroom. The sink then the shower and the spigot in the bath tub. They too were dry.

Odd. Where was the dripping tap?

He turned on the bathroom light.

Normally his night vision was sufficient for him to move around in a darkened room, even a pitch black one, but he needed to find that dripping tap if he was going to get any more sleep tonight.

He had an important sales meeting tomorrow and his boss, Mr. Walters, would be very unhappy if he missed the meeting. The Tri-State Automotive Parts and Repo account was the crème de la crème in his company. As vice-president of sales it was his job to keep this important client happy.

They bought seventy percent of the replacement lamps for auto headlights that his company Steven Lamps sold, and if they lost the account then most of the current jobs in the company? Mr Walters would of course fire him if he failed.

Why am I always getting distracted by such minor crap as dripping taps when there're are far more important things to worry about?

Will stood over his Samsonite suitcase sitting open atop the stand he'd unfolded when he'd arrived.

He selected a pair of swim trunks his wife, Maggie had packed for him. Not that he had time to swim, but she always said he should be prepared for anything.

He slipped first one leg then the other into the purple and orange nylon trunks then pulled the suit up past his narrow hips to his waist.

Drip

His naturally dark curls were flattened by the pillow and the perspiration had so twisted his hair out of its natural shape he was certain he looked sufficiently scary to anyone he might meet outside. He paused to listen. In the silence he heard the unmistakable dripping, rhythmic pattern drumming away to its own beat.

He sighed and then slipped his tanned simulated leather walking shoes over his bare feet. He thought of putting on a shirt, but decided not to bother. The night was warm and he'd only be out of the room for a few minutes anyway.

He stepped onto the covered wood walkway outside his room and was greeted by a burst of crickets chirping happily greeting him.

Great. More noisy critters to keep me awake the rest of the night.

He hesitated.

Funny, why didn't I hear them before now? They must've been here. Maybe I just didn't notice them.

Will moved toward the stairs leading to the ground floor and the parking lot beyond.

He made sure the door was closed firmly by pulling hard on the imitation brass doorknob. The sound of the dripping tap seemed louder in the direction of the parking lot.

There was a single streetlight illuminating the parking lot. The blub cast a faded burnt orange color across the hot pavement. Will knew his lamps and bulbs so he knew when one needed replacing.

As he reached the top of the stairs he could see the motel's office with its darkened windows and shredded curtains hanging like cheesecloth on either side of the window. There were three other vehicles besides his in the parking lot. A white Buick Century, a silver Jeep, and a black Ford pickup parked in separate corners of the lot. The air was rife with the odor of gas and oil.

His '87 Skylark wagon was the farthest away. He'd had the car for years. Due to its two hundred plus thousand miles it wasn't worth much to anyone but him. It was the one possession he loved more than Maggie. Not that he'd ever tell her.

The dripping echoed from the foot of the stairs ahead. Once at the top of the staircase he spotted a rain trough with an old-fashioned hand pump hung over it he surmised must originate at an underground well.

He walked down the rickety wooden stairs. The worn stairs creaked sharply with every step. He winced with every footfall.

Please don't collapse now.

Glancing toward the office he was startled to see what was obviously a light from a flashlight in the motel office's windows. He paused and held his breath afraid he'd woken another light sleeper like himself.

The yellow beam of light from the flashlight moved round the room pausing as if someone were searching for something.

He shrugged. Whoever it was it was none of his business.

He continued down the stairs until he reached the cracked cement pad at the base. He approached the rain trough.

It was constructed from an old oil drum cut in half then soldered together to form the trough. Sure enough the pump spout was dripping slowly splashing against the side of steel drum with a deafening splatter. At least it seemed deafening to him.

The drum half's were rusted away at the bottom so whatever water attempted to accumulate leaked into the ground beneath the barrel.

Will gazed at the pump handle and saw that it was stuck partly open.

That explained why it was dripping. He placed one hand on the pump handle and pushed hard but it didn't budge. It had obviously rusted in place some time ago.

Odd, why did it start to drip only now?

He gripped the handle in both hands and

struggled to move it. After nearly popping his hernia he managed to close the lever. Beads of sweat now covered his lean frame. He was gasping for breath.

The dripping had finally stopped. Mission accomplished.

Will smirked and rubbed his hands together in satisfaction. It was only then he noticed his hands were covered in orange rust, and the metallic smell made him a little nauseous. He definitely wasn't cut out for manual labour.

He glanced toward the office again and saw the beam from the flashlight was gone. The owner of the flashlight should've changed the bulb in that baby a long time ago. Even with fresh batteries the bulb was going to burn out very soon. He knew his bulbs.

He shook his head and headed back to the wooden stairs to return to his room. He'd be able to sleep now. He paused at the bottom of the stairs. The crickets had gone silent again.

Good, I'll get some sleep after all.

He hurried up the stairs, accompanied by the musical creaks the boards protesting under his weight. Finally he arrived at the door to his room. He turned the door handle only to find the door locked.

He tried it again without success. *I must've locked it out of habit.*

He patted down the pockets of his swim trunks and realized he didn't have the key. Now, he'd have to wake the old man and ask for a spare key. His face felt warm as embarrassment swept over him.

He was nearly naked in the middle of the night. How would he explain what he was doing out here at this hour? A grown man kept awake by a dripping tap. The old guy would think he'd lost his marbles.

The Vice President of sales wasn't supposed to get himself into such dilemmas. What would Mr. Walters think if he saw him right now?

Will sighed and chuckled. If Walters were here he would of course fire him. But his boss was hundreds of miles away.

When Walters bought the company from Maggie's father, Hiram W. Steven, one of the conditions of the sale was that his son-in-law be guaranteed a job for as long as he wanted it. Walters had been itching to find a way to rid of Will ever since that day five years ago. Now Walters may have the excuse he needed.

If he ever found out, which he wouldn't.

He retraced his steps to the top of the staircase and peered through the gloom into the motel's darkened office.

The bulb inside the street lamp was blinking intermittently now threatening to go out altogether.

Will hurried down the stairs barely noticing the creaking this time. The crickets were still silent as if they were waiting for something.

As Will stepped to the cement pad at the foot of the stairs the parking lot and the motel were abruptly plunged into inky darkness. With a burst of light as bright as a camera's flash going off the street lamp had finally gone out. There was no moon.

The only light available now was the sea of stars overhead. Will waited until his eyes adjusted to the meagre light. His night vision kicked in and soon he was able to find his way to the office. As he neared the office door he noticed it was slightly ajar.

Odd. Things that were odd were beginning to pile up. I've a bad feeling about this.

He stepped to the door and pushed on it lightly with his finger tips. The surface of the wood felt like it had been freshly painted. The door swung open noiselessly on well-oiled hinges.

Maybe the old guy was finally fixing up the place? Will shrugged. About time.

The office was in total darkness. Taking in a breath he stepped inside nearly tripping over something lying on the floor.

It was a large lump that looked vaguely familiar to him. He dropped to rest on his haunches to study the lump more closely. He gasped when he realized the shape was human.

His breath caught in his throat and his heart began to beat faster. Maybe it was a dead body? His mouth dried. He licked his dry lips. Oh, crap. I don't feel so good.

He rested one hand on the floor to steady himself and his fingers touched something sticky and warm. He froze with a rush of fear. Was that blood? The smell of iron filled his nostrils. A wave of nausea came over him. He stood up like a shot and panic raced through his mind.

What should I do?

He stood for what seemed like an eternity glued to the floor his mind racing with possibilities. The flashlight person must've been the killer. Maybe he was still around here somewhere.

Squinting in the darkness Will could make out the reception desk.

That's it. I'll call the cops. They'll know what to do.

He hurried to the reception desk his trembling hands fumbled around until he found the telephone. It was one of those old dial type phones.

10

He hadn't seen one of those in years. He lifted the receiver to his ear and heard the thundering sound of silence.

A bead of sweat trickled down his back. The starlight coming through the front door was the only illumination. He could make out the body of the old man now lying on his side. He recognized the thin sweater the guy had on when he'd first seen him.

Will's eyes went wide when the old man moaned and rolled on his back his arms falling wide away from his wizened body. He was still alive.

Will dropped the receiver onto the desk. It landed with a thud. He then quickly moved to kneel beside the old man. "Are you okay?" he said his voice shaking.

Will rolled his eyes. I'm an idiot. Of course the old man wasn't okay.

The old man must have been shot or stabbed or something. And if the attacker was still nearby then he might be next.

Will decided to return to his room and barricade himself inside until help arrived. He paused. He couldn't leave the old man here. He might bleed to death.

From what he recalled during those monotonous first aid courses, Mr. Walters made him attend at the plant with the assembly line workers, Will knew he shouldn't move an injured man.

But then again what choice did he have? The old man would die here regardless.

Will moved behind the old man and lifted him by his armpits. Blowing out his cheeks and puffing he managed to raise the old man enough so he could drag him by his heels.

The old man was like a dead weight but he managed to drag him outside the office. The old man moaned softly as he dragged him.

Once outside, Will eased him to the ground. Then bent over at the waist and drew in deep breaths, his arms trembling from the exertion and the sweat pouring off him.

Manual labour really isn't one my strengths.

When his breathing became somewhat regular he again reached under the old man's arms and began to drag him to the foot of the stairs where he once again eased him to the ground.

As he struggled to catch his breath he gazed around and was assured to see he was alone. The silence surrounding him was suddenly not as welcoming as it had once been.

In the last several minutes it was if as if his world had suddenly been turned upside down.

From his stooped position he lifted his eyes to gaze at the stairs before him.

It might as well be Everest.

He wondered how he would get the old man up those stairs. The old man had stopped moaning, but he could see the man's chest rising and falling so he knew he was still alive.

"Here goes nothing," he murmured under his breath.

He reached under the old man's arms and heaved him up. He shifted the dead weight until it felt about the right balance then backed toward the stairs.

He managed to gradually climb up the stairs one by one. The squeak of the tortured echo off the buildings surrounding the parking lot. As he climbed he looked over at the lot and nearly dropped the old man. He counted the vehicles. One was missing.

The silver Jeep was gone. How could that be? He hadn't heard an engine start while he was in the office. He looked around frantically as he negotiated the last few steps and arrived at the top of the stairs. His thin arms trembled as he eased the old man onto the deck then collapsed to his knees breathing hard, partly with excretion, partly with fear.

Something was wrong about all this. His instincts were sending him warning signals.

It was like that time Ernie Walls wanted him to ride with him and Harold to the soda shop when he was seventeen. His two friends died in the car accident on Highway Seven when Ernie's brakes failed. Somehow he knew something was wrong and said that he didn't want to go with them.

It was no time to stop now they were almost at the room. He rose to his feet and again grasped the old man and began again to drag him to the room down the walkway. A soft moan escaped the old man's lips.

"Shush," whispered Will. His voice sounded harsh to his ears, but the old man stopped moaning right away.

He stopped outside his room door and eased the man to the thin, rough all-weather carpet covering the two-by-fours of the walkway. It occurred to him the worn carpet smelled of oil.

Again another irrelevant fact. He grimaced at the thought.

Maybe Mr. Walters was right. Maybe he should quit before he was fired. He could always go back to selling used cars. It was something he'd done to pay his way through business school.

He'd not been the most successful car salesman but he'd managed to leave school debt free. All things considered he'd done okay.

Maggie's father had offered him the job at Steven Lamp based on his track record at the car dealer so it certainly counted for something didn't it?

Will reached for the doorknob when he realized he forgotten to get the spare key from the office. Now he'd have to go back and get it.

With one back of one hand he wiped the rivulets of sweat running down his face and contemplated his next move. He shrugged. He would just have to risk going back to the office for the key.

If only the old man were conscious he wouldn't have to search the place to find the spare keys to the rooms.

When he'd checked in the old man had disappeared into a backroom and reappeared with the key in hand. It had one of those oval shaped moulded plastic key holders attached with the name and address of the motel engraved on it and a request to drop it in the nearest mailbox if found.

His options were limited. He left the old man unconscious outside his door and headed again for the stairs. He just made it to the ground level when suddenly night turned into day.

He was surrounded by a powerful beam of white light. He closed his eyes to the dazzling light and was frozen in place like a fly caught in amber.

He raised one hand to shield his tearing eyes from the blinding white light just as he heard the roar of a motor spring to life. The growl of the obviously powerful engine was off to his left.

His instincts told him whoever was behind those headlights wasn't a friendly. He recalled the general direction of the office and decided to make a break for it. He could've gone back up the stairs, but with his suddenly limited eyesight he probably have tripped and broken something on the way up. It had to be the office.

He broke into a run. His legs felt as if they were mired in quicksand. The effort he'd expended carrying to old man up the stairs had made them weak.

The engine noise increased followed by the sound of tires spinning on the gravel. There was a roar of an engine. The vehicle was headed at me? Why?

His heart pounded in his chest. He blinked to clear his vision and was thankful when the office door was much closer than he'd thought it was.

In sheer desperation he launched himself into the air and landed heavily on his stomach knocking the wind out of him but realized he'd landed on a carpeted floor.

I made it!

He rolled over and gasped draging heated air into his tortured lungs.

There was a sudden the crunch of metal and splintering of wood as the vehicle that had been chasing him crashed into the doorway behind him.

Will covered his head with his arms. Oh, crap. What the....

The office was suddenly flooded with bright white headlights followed by the sound of a car horn stuck on. The engine gasped, coughed roughly then died. The bleating car horn continued.

Will's head swam and he lost consciousness.

***

When Will woke he found a smiling male face above him looking at him. The man wore a blue pin striped suit and matching tie over a white shirt. His cherubic clean shaven features, replete with rosy cheeks, and flashing hazel eyes crinkled at the corners.

Is this was my maker looks like? He gazed into the friendly face.

"How are you feeling, Mr. Aston?" said his maker.

Will then noticed a shiny gold badge in a black leather wallet sticking out of the left breast pocket of the man's suit. This was a cop not his maker. Another stupid idea.

"Huh…okay, I guess…" Actually he felt like he'd run a marathon.

Not that he knew what that felt like, but his muscles ached and his head hurt so he assumed it. He was lying on a soft bed. He realized it was an ambulance stretcher.

"Do you think you can answer a few questions?" said the cop. "I'm Detective Zale."

"Yeah…I think so." It was really the last thing he wanted to do right now, but what choice did he have?

"Good," said Zale. The cop pulled out a leather encased brown notebook from his suit pocket. He flipped some pages back pausing to study some of his notes. His chubby features were transformed by the occasional frown. Zale then smiled slightly as he shifted his gaze back to Will.

"Do you know a Ronald Walters?"

Will nodded. "Yeah…huh…he's my boss…"

"Was," interrupted Zale with a slight smirk.

Will's eyes went wide. Mr. Walters? What happened? "What do you mean?"

"Sorry to break the news to you, pal he's dead. In fact, he tried to run you down with that Jeep."

Zale nodded to the door to the motel's office, which was framed by sunlight. There in the center of the doorway was the crumpled shaped of the silver Jeep he'd seen in the parking lot last night.

R.G. Crossley

Its front grill and hood were twisted out of shape as it someone had taken a sledgehammer to it.

"I don't understand...." said Will.

Zale continued in his matter-of-fact way.

"From what we can tell Walters came here last night hoping to murder you. He knocked out the manager of the place, then tried to run you down with the Jeep." Zale paused and looked thoughtful. "Something I don't understand though why were you out here in your swim trunks? This motel doesn't have a pool."

My boss...tried to kill me?

Somehow, Walters found out about him being an extremely light sleeper, so he must've turned on the dripping tap knowing it would wake him.

Walters couldn't very well sneak into his room without drawing attention to himself so he'd waited until the motel was quiet then made sure the pump handle was open just enough to cause a drip.

Then he'd waited for him to come down and turn it off. The manager must've heard him and come to investigate and Walters knocked him unconscious.

"How's the old man?" said Will suddenly worried about the old guy.

Zale waved away his concern is if he were shooing flies.

"Don't worry about him. He's at County General. They tell me he's gonna be fine. He's a strong old bugger. And smart too."

Will gave him a quizzical look. Zale chuckled lightly, his sandpaper coloured eyes dancing.

"He'd just replaced the doorframe to the office with steel reinforced beams. They've had a number of break-ins around here and they'd lost some cash so he was in the process of renovating the office to prevent thieves from jimmying the door. Good thing for you. Otherwise that Jeep would've shredded the wooden frame as if it were tissue paper…"

A blond haired male cop in his neatly pressed brown sheriff's uniform interrupted Zale to whisper something in his right ear. Zale looked surprised. His bushy eyebrows arched on his forehead.

"Are you sure?" The blond nodded his expression grim then he turned and walked away leaving them alone.

Zale turned back to face Will looking embarrassed his cheeks were crimson. "Mr. Aston, we've identified the other victim in the Jeep…"

"There was someone else with him? Who?"

"Margaret Aston."

A wave of shock wahsed over Will like a tidal wave.

Maggie? Maggie was involved in this mess? How could that be?

The emergency sales trip was a ruse. Maggie and Walters must've been lovers and they wanted him out of the way.

How could I be so stupid, so blind?

He thought back and realized it explained everything. How else would Walters know he was such a light sleeper? They were both dead. They'd paid for their betrayal with their lives.

"All this from a drip," he murmured.

"What?" said Zale.

"Nothing — nothing important."

A Perfect Crime

BIG PETE SCRATCHED his butt absentmindedly as he stood in the crowded subway train headed uptown. An elderly lady seated behind him made an ewww noise he ignored.

Teleporters were too expensive on his limited income. He was forced to rely on the squeaking, bone-rattling cattle cars that made up the subway as his transportation of choice (or lack of choice).

These days every subway car was filled to the max with a seething, stinking mass of humanity all day long. The so-called rush-hours of the past were just that, they were in the past.

He smirked. "This here's a condition that's gonna change, and soon," he mused. His fingers tightened around the briefcase's handle in his right hand.

A Perfect Crime

"What's so funny, man?" said a greasy-haired, meghead standing next to him. The puke's sweaty armpit was almost in Pete's face. He had the appearance of one of those punks who was plugged into a heavy metal I-Pod Implant to listen to his music all day. If you could call that noise music.

Pete preferred the classics; the Stones, Marvin Gaye, Avril Lavagine. Any music was preferable to the junk this kid no doubt listened to twenty-four-seven.

The purple rooster ridge atop the punk's smooth pink head looked like implants. Or maybe his hair had been genetically altered prior to birth. Who knew anymore, and more important why would he care?

"Nuthin' that's any of yore bizness, punk-ass," said Big Pete, his inky gaze traveling up and down the younger man as if he was eyeing a sidewalk turd.

The younger man's eyes shifted to a look of concern. It had obviously dawned on him he had no idea who he was talking to. And while he was a head taller than Big Pete the older man's arms were heavily muscled, and his wide chest stretched his tight dirt-brown tee shirt to reveal the ridges of an equally muscled torso.

Pete fought the urge to chuckle at the guy while he kept his eyes fixed on the younger man's face that was becoming visibly paler with each passing second.

Pete always enjoyed the way blood ran from the face of anyone who challenged him.

"Sumthin' wrong?" asked Pete.

The punk shook his head then averted his eyes to stare at the floor of the subway car.

Pete smirked again and went back to thinking about his part in Armand's plan. It was the perfect plan for a perfect crime.

***

Pete arrived outside the Excitement Corporation towers whistling a Stones tune to anyone who had no choice but to listen. He was off key as usual, but he didn't care. Naturally, he failed to notice passersby who lacked an appreciation of his musical talents.

He stopped and gazed upward at the sixty stories of glass and steel tower that housed the world headquarters of the company that was about to define his future. And make him and the others the richest people on the planet.

He entered through a set of revolving glass doors and made his way to the executive elevators to the left of the two identical rows of regular lifts. These were the ones reserved for company executives.

A burly guard, replete with regulation crew cut, and a well pressed blue and gray uniform, stood with his large muscular arms crossed over his massive chest.

His bright blue eyes were fixed on the fireplug-shaped male headed for his position. Pete saw the slight twitch of the guard's neck muscles. This was the signal to his backup to join him right away.

Good for him, thought Pete. He smells trouble with a capital T when he sees it.

As he arrived in front of the guard Pete forced a wide smile across his swarthy complexion. "Hi."

"Sir." The guard nodded keeping his eyes fixed on Pete's. His large hands were folded over each other in front of him as if he were guarding his family jewels. "May I help you," said the guard, the timber of his voice surprisingly high-pitched. His eyes were narrow as Pete watched the man's arms tense, and his booted-feet make those small measured moves to plant himself as if he were a human version of the classic brick wall.

"Big Pete Rustica to see Armand Takly."

The guard's thick dark eyebrows rose slightly upward on his dusky forehead. Pete knew that was because he wasn't the usual class of visitor that visited the Vice-President of Development for the largest Personal Recreational Interface Experience manufacturer in the world. The PRIE was the first and best system ever made.

It was the Blu Ray to the DVD of this generation. Brilliant marketing and a fairly reliable system of making customers dreams come true had made tens of billions of dollars in profits for everyone involved.

Armand Takly had been the chief systems architect of this technological miracle, and rumor was he was about to be arrested on trumped up fraud charges. When he was convicted — as he most certainly would be — his stock options would be revoked. And his bank accounts would be raped, leaving him a penniless pauper rotting in a jail cell.

Not that Armand wasn't guilty.

Every corporate executive was guilty of something. It was just that Armand thought he was made of Teflon, untouchable. He made the mistake of trusting his partners in crime.

Unbeknownst to his enemies, Armand had a safety net. His spies were in every boardroom and office in the company. He had his own plans to become very, very, very rich in the process. But he needed help.

This was where Big Pete, Tiny Murdoch, and Maurice "The Leech" Lévesque came into the picture.

When they were kids Maurice, and Armand attended school together in a small village in France.

A Perfect Crime

A fact scrubbed from company records, because if the company found out he was once associated with a notorious jewel thief he would never get away with what they were about to attempt.

Safety nets were important.

Maurice had never been caught — or even under suspicion by the authorities — for his illegal activities. Consequently, he could travel with complete anonymity anywhere in the world. Big Pete and Tiny were the worker bees of this operation.

They did all the heavy lifting and were well compensated for their part of the many successful robberies planned and executed by Maurice and his team.

The expert thief's policy was to steal from the rich who kept their valuables off the books. Insurance agents and the police wouldn't be looking for the perpetrators of the crimes. They didn't even have any idea where to begin looking if they pulled off each heist as planned.

It was a convenient and lucrative operation for all involved.

Of course, this didn't guarantee there weren't people looking for them. Many of these rich people were upset about losing their valuable trinkets. They would send private contractors to investigate.

So far, no one had gotten close to the truth.

The truth was the rich victims often bought back their own merchandise at the next high priced auction even though the pieces looked very different from how they had last seen them.

Ironic, eh what? thought Pete with amusement.

He stood next to the cowed guard riding upward to the top floor in the high-speed elevator. When the guard checked with Armand's office the Vice President's personal assistant growled at him to stop delaying Mr. Rustica.

The elevator car was rife with the scent of the guard's cologne. It reminded Pete of rose water.

Kinda girly for a big guy like him. But what the hell. I'm not his mother.

The office over looked the city through a wall of glass spread out like a shining monument to man's ingenuity. The view took Pete's breath away. He had never been this high over the city.

Armand sat behind his glass desk. Tiny and Maurice sat in shiny red leather wing chairs in front of Armand's desk. Armand looked so regal in his five thousand dollar custom made suit. His black hair was streaked with traces of gray.

His weathered face broke into a smile as Peter entered the room followed by Armand's assailant, a comely redhead dressed in a beige pantsuit who smelled of green apples.

"Thank you, Miss Taylor, please get a chair for Mr. Rustica —"

"Call me Pete, please," said Pete to Armand as Miss Taylor lifted and carried, with one hand, another of the red leather chairs away from where it sat against a wall then set it down next to Tiny's chair.

Impressive. Pete admired the woman's upper body strength. She probably doubled as Armand's bodyguard. Having a bodyguard that's easy on the eyes is a rich man's bonus.

Soon I'll be able to afford five who look like her.

Tiny's amused gaze followed Miss Taylor's rear end as she turned and left the room closing the door to the outer office behind her.

"My, my," breathed Tiny.

"Knock it off, Tiny," said Pete jokingly. "Ya'll soon be fightin' broads like her off with yore big stick."

Tiny snorted. "I'll show her a big stick awright —" To punctuate his point he grabbed his crotch.

"Will you two please cease the juvenile banter. We have serious work ahead," said Maurice dryly.

Pete and Tiny looked at each other and shrugged.

I hate it when he talks all high and mighty in fronta clients.

Some guys would think he was puttin' 'em down for not bein' so educated. Of course, Maurice and us we been makin' a lotta dough together over the years so he must be jokin'. If there's one thing I'm good at it's readin' people."

"You bring the item?" said Armand, his tone anxious.

Pete wanted to laugh aloud, but he managed to contain himself. "Yeah. I have the item."

Guy musta seen one too many movies. Dork.

Pete slapped the hard-shelled black leather briefcase on the desk. He thumbed the catches on the left and right of the handle and they popped loudly with a metal-on-metal snap in the silence of the office.

Pete picked the data chip from a pouch designed to store and protect it then handed it to Maurice. A small plastic disk — about the size of a large washer — contained five trillion megabytes of data within its memory.

"Is this the one we need? As we discussed?" asked Armand.

Pete was getting seriously irritated by the guy, but he nodded any way forcing a placid expression to his face.

A Perfect Crime

Maurice must have detected Pete's annoyance because he said, "As we agreed this simulation will allow us to practice the robbery countless times until we have it perfected —"

"How long will it take — I don't have a lot of time you know —"

Maurice held up one hand to silence his old school chum. Armand went quiet his eyes flitting back and forth over the three men sitting across from him.

Maurice cleared his throat then said, "We need the big lab on the seventh floor. It will take ten days to practice, then two to affect the robbery. The cops will buzz like angry hornets for several weeks afterward, but I'm not concerned with them. By the time they piece together what happened we'll be in a neutral country, safe from prosecution."

"Are there any neutral countries anymore?" said Armand.

A crooked smile crossed Maurice's face and his dark eyes flashed with humor. His fine boned hands smoothed his slate-gray dress slacks and he rolled his shoulders slightly beneath his gray tweed sport coat. "But of course, my old friend. I know all the right people in all the low places."

Armand eased back in his executive chair and laughed.

Pete stole a glance at Tiny. They both shrugged seemingly uncomprehending. What the heck were the two men were talking about? They were off the books. They weren't going anywhere as far as Pete was concerned.

***

Pete materialized within the walls of the vault. He stood frozen in place for a moment until the containment beam dissipated. Good thing too. If the quantum computer didn't reassemble your molecules in just the right place it was goodbye world and hello oblivion.

He looked around amazed at what he was seeing. It all looked so real. The vault even smelled of money. How freakin' real do these things get.

He'd always thought the PRIE's were designed for high-end gamers. Those types didn't need to steal. They just played at crime. It wasn't very long ago when people thought a video game could make someone commit a crime. Morons. The idea was just plain stupid.

Of course, the PRIE was much more than those old passive game systems. The gamer actually was able to interact with characters and change the outcome of the game.

A Perfect Crime

Safety systems were designed so the user wouldn't be hurt, but gamers could be shot, stabbed, or blown to bits, or make love to the woman of their dreams. It seemed as real to the gamer as the real world.

"Talk about your safe sex," Pete mused.

What you couldn't use the system for was to commit a crime. Even a simulated crime like the one they were attempting. A black lab — one that would create anything for anyone for a price — created the program they were using to test the robbery. The lone downside was the safety protocols had to be taken out. Even holo-bullets can kill.

Oh well. Who wants to live forever?

Real people didn't have a use for such expensive toys. Million-billionaires bought these things. While there were plenty of them around Pete and Tiny certainly weren't in that category. The most they'd ever made in one year of working for Maurice was a hundred grand. Certainly not enough to buy an SUV never mind one of these expensive gadgets.

Armand's money paid for the black lab version and Pete knew it had taken most of his available cash. No wonder the guy was desperate. It was all or nothing. A real crapshoot. As it was for them.

They had never been on the cops radar given the attention this job was going to draw it would have to be their last. In the real vault, the hidden monitors couldn't be bypassed so their images would be flashed around the world when the robbery was discovered. They would just have to ensure they left the country ahead of the cops. Simple.

Yeah, right.

Of course, they planned to use the toy for far more than its designers originally intended.

They ran the robbery simulation seventeen times without one successful test.

The plan involved using a teleporter to materialize inside the vault containing the patents for every known piece of new tech that was acquired during contact with the Vetsa.

The Vetsa was an alien race that willingly shared their technology with Earth's industrialists. What the aliens didn't bargain on was the ruthlessness of Earth's most ambitious men and women.

The super rich wiped out all life on the aliens home world using their own technology and weapons. Not humanities finest hour.

A consortium of industrialists quickly applied for patents for the alien tech.

A Perfect Crime

Humans now had access to teleporters, flying cars, guns that were encoded to one person's brain chemistry, and this holo-technology. The Personal Recreation Interface Entertainment (or PRIE) system made it possible to simulate any environment programmed by the user. Science fiction was now science reality.

Pete released the strap that held his .45 in place and held it up as the door to the outer vault area slide rapidly open and two guards rushed in wearing body armor. Pete methodically killed them both with one shot each in the center of their forehead. They dropped like two sacks of potatoes landing with hard thumps onto the tiled floor. Their drawn pistols skittered across the ties to stop at Pete's feet.

The iron scent of blood penetrated the air masking the smell of the money.

During the first two simulations, the two sim-guards had surprised him grazing his left shoulder in the resulting shoot out. He failed to notice they were wearing protective vests and had shot them each in the chest.

This slowed them but they kept coming and it had taken him several seconds to realize his mistake and take them down. Pain and the sight of your own blood were good teachers. He had to agree with Maurice. He was lucky.

Pete stepped over the two pistols just as Tiny materialized. He was wearing the body pack with the C4. Working quickly the two men squeezed the C4 from its packaging onto the center two titanium lined safety deposit boxes. The stuff looked like plumbers putty, but with more of a kick.

The boxes were eighteen inches by eighteen inches square. The patent certificates were secured inside. Pete licked his dry lips as they finished then he stuck in the detonators and set the timers for ten seconds.

He nodded to Tiny and they pressed their recall buttons simultaneously. The two thieves dematerialized and were standing on the lab floor looking at the large monitor affixed to one wall.

Within seconds, the screen became distorted, and as was the case seventeen times before, the floor beneath their feet trembled from the force of the blast. The screen settled down once more. Gray smoke obscured their view until powerful air exchange fans designed to remove smoke in case of fire sucked the smoke from the vault room.

Tiny glanced at Pete and smiled knowingly.

The two thieves pressed the buttons on their belts again and in the blink of an eye stood in the hazy air of the vault were looking at two safety despots boxes split open like fresh cantaloupe.

Instinctively Tiny reached inside the box nearest him. He froze and his face visibly paled. He stumbled backward holding his damaged hand. The boxes were booby-trapped.

Tiny groaned and blood dripped onto the floor from his nearly severed hand. There was a large gash across the back of his hand cutting through the skin exposing the bone in his wrist.

This wasn't good. If Tiny's blood was found inside the real vault his DNA would lead the cops right to him. Could Tiny stand up to interrogation? Or would he talk to save his own skin?

Pete wasn't certain. Nope this 'isn't good.

"Hold." Pete and Tiny materialized back in the lab facing a distraught Armand and a very worried looking Maurice. Peter had never seen his boss look so worried.

"You okay, boss?" asked Pete. Stupid question, Peter. Moron.

"Very funny, Pete —" Tiny hit the floor hard and lay still. He'd lost a lot of blood and had no doubt fainted.

"What about him?" asked Pete, gazing at his friend laying unconscious on the floor curled in the fetal position.

"Take him to the infirmary on the first floor," said Armand curtly.

Pete shrugged and bent down to gather Tiny in his massive arms. He cradled him like a baby and then headed for the elevators.

***

"Test Nineteen," Pete said into the mike.

Within microseconds the massive computing power of the quantum computer than ran PRIE, the teleporter simultaneously set up the simulation, and he dematerialized.

As before, once in the vault he shot the two guards as if he was shooting at aluminum ducks at the carnival then set the charges and the timers.

Once the smoke from the explosion cleared, Pete stood staring at the two boxes. One contained a deadly trap that killed his friend — unbeknownst to them the blades in the trap were tipped with puffer fish venom — Tiny hadn't fainted he'd died. The other contained the certificates that were worth limitless wealth. They would be kings of all they surveyed.

For the first time in his life the question Pete faced was is this worth it?

Closing his eyes, he ignored the box Tiny had put his hand in and instead reached inside the other one.

Nothing happened until his fingers brushed over paper. Hen snapped back his hand. His eyes flew open and frantically inspected his appendage for damage.

With a deep sense of relief, he let out the breath he'd been holding and felt the urge to laugh.

Finally.

He quickly reached inside and pulled out the sim-certificates then slapped the button on his belt with the flat of his hand. Nothing happened so this time he gingerly pressed the button again.

Again, nothing.

What the — ?

An alarm began to wail and a wall of steel bars appeared from the ceiling blocking his exit via the door the two dead guards had come through.

Something was seriously wrong.

"Ah, Mr. Rustica I presume," said a deep baritone voice on the opposite side of the bars.

Pete walked toward the man his pistol drawn held waist level in front of him. Standing with an arrogant smirk on his lips on the other side of the bars was a man of medium height and weight wearing the uniform of the secret police.

In his youth, Pete had been a member of that organization so he knew the attire well. He also recognized the insignia on the collar. The man with the brown nearly trimmed beard, shot through with gray streaks, was a colonel.

"I hate officers," Pete murmured.

"I seem to have the drop on you, colonel," said Pete waving the pistol to emphasize his point.

The colonel chuckled and crossed his arms over his chest. "Yes. I believe you do at that, Mr. Rustica —"

"Call me Pete."

"And you can call me Colonel Driver, Pete."

Pete feigned surprise. "Why so formal, Driver?"

Colonel Driver frowned. "Well you see, Pete, you and I are going to be spending a lot of time together."

It was Pete's turn to laugh. "I don't think so, Colonel. As you can see I have the gun."

Out of the corner of one eye, Pete saw a blur of movement coming from behind him. He attempted to turn but was too late. He felt a hard, painful snap against the back of his head and he fell on his side to the floor. His world exploded in a dizzying array of lights and spots that danced across his vision.

Dazed but still conscious he looked up at the Colonel who was now standing over him the bars having retreated into the ceiling.

"I don't understand," gasped Pete weakly. He detected the scent of the waxy polish coming from Drivers gleaming, calf-height boots.

"You're a deserter. You were convicted in abstentia by a military court. You will be taken into custody and serve your life sentence in Leavenworth."

A Perfect Crime

"I have rights —"

"Deserters have no rights."

"But I committed the perfect crime."

"Mr. Rustica, there is no such thing as the perfect crime." Driver's eyes flashed. "Especially when a grief stricken woman is involved."

Pete's eyes looked puzzled.

Driver smiled mirthlessly. "Miss Taylor is one of our agents. She tipped us off what you and the others were doing. We're not interested in prosecution of the thievery, but I think you'll find your partners in crime will all be resting comfortably as wards of the state for quite some time."

Pete felt two sets of strong hands grab his arms and lift him from the floor. His feet dragged so the two cops each held him up by placing one of his arms over their shoulders. They each had one around his waist to support his weight.

Driver was about to walk away when he paused and appeared thoughtful.

"And one more thing," he said slowly. "We would never have found out about you without Tiny Murdoch's death. I'm truly sorry about him, but as the French say, 'Ce la vie.'

"Of course, the real loser in this little drama is Miss Taylor. She truly loved Tiny."

The Apprentice

SIX WEEKS.

They spent six weeks planning the mission and the last thing he expected was a queasy stomach after all that time.

Ignoring his discomfort, Perrin ripped the strip of gray duct tape off the roll he had so meticulously pre-cut. This meant little effort was needed to pull off a strip just the right length.

The odor of the glue filled his nostrils forcing him sniff to try and clear the chemical smell from his nose and mouth. Like a bombardier centering the cross hairs on his target, he carefully applied the tape over the loose hanging mouth. He then pressed the tape hard into the soft flesh on either side of the mouth.

The Apprentice

Its eyes remained closed, but the chest continuing to rise and fall was a sure sign of the familiar rhythm of sleep.

This sleep was artificially induced with the aid of the no-name chloroform he had purchased at Walgreen's, but it was still asleep.

They would need to wake it to complete their mission.

Perrin glanced up at the perspiration-dotted bald head of his father bent over it tying the knotted white rope around its pale wrists he had bought at Home Depot.

The rope was thin but strong. It was impossible to break unless you were big Arnold. This pudgy female with grey streaks shot through her artificially curled hair certainly didn't look like the strong type.

He could still detect the peroxide odor from the perm solution used to make its hair curly. Standing this close to it the new smell masked the trace odors left by the chloroform. Another very good reason to end its existence.

This was Perrin's first time since agreeing to become his father's apprentice.

He hadn't seen his Dad — he liked the sound of that word, 'Dad' because it filled him with a warmth unlike any he'd experienced toward anything or anyone for as long as could recall — since Dad and Mom deserted him years ago.

It had been a complete surprise when his father approached him at his $5.50-an-hour job at the Whistle Burger in the mall.

Since he didn't know the old man, he was neither happy to see him, nor angry with him.

He just didn't know this bald, heavy-jowled man so he also didn't care one way or the other.

He barely recognized the craggy features of the man from the pictures he kept in the tattered cardboard cigar box he carried with him as he moved from foster home to foster home while growing up. But it was the eyes that provided a clue to the man's identity.

Eyes the color of a cloudy sky were free of any emotion. It was as if the old man were death itself.

Yup, those eyes were a feature you could never mistake even from a picture.

When his father came to him he offered him an apprentice position with the telephone company where Oslo Hollis had worked for thirty years.

The Apprentice

It took six months of working with Oslo and accompanying him on all sorts of service calls in his telephone company service truck before Oslo revealed his true intent.

Of course, Perrin had begun to suspect something strange was going on after Oslo caught him watching a documentary on television about a serial killer called the Smile Killer.

Perrin would never forget Oslo's burst of anger and demand he never watch such things again. Perrin's inner voice said Oslo's reaction was far more than parental concern for his not-so delicate sensibilities.

It was only when Perrin found the knife in Oslo's toolbox did he truly begin to suspect that his father was involved in something much more sinister than servicing telephones.

Naturally, Perrin burned to say something – in fact, he was bursting inside to say something, but he kept his suspicions bottled up inside. Until finally, Oslo said something over dinner one night.

Father and son sat silently eating across the small kitchen table from each other, their eyes avoiding the others. Sitting on the table in front of each of them was a microwave-heated TV dinner consisting of thinly sliced roast beef, peas and carrots, whipped potatoes, and apple cobbler.

Perrin had just popped some of the stringy beef into his mouth when he glanced up and saw his father was picking at his food.

Perrin paused and asked, "What's wrong, Dad?"

His father winced. "It's that obvious?"

Perrin put his fork down next to the aluminum tray and swallowed the piece of microwaved beef swimming in the bland gravy. "Yeah."

Oslo's emotionless gaze locked on his son's intense gaze. "I have something to tell you. Something important..."

Now this was getting interesting.

Perrin leaned forward his arms resting flat on the table his hands also flat on the table as if grounding himself. The sound of the cat-faced clock with its cheery smile hanging on the wall next to the white fridge seemed to be ticking louder in the thick silence that suddenly descended upon the room. His heart beat hard against his ribs as his excitement grew.

"I am..." Oslo hesitated. "I've never told anyone..."

"You can trust me, Da —"

Perrin felt a strange glow surge from his toes up his belly, landing finally in his throat where it choked his words off. He didn't want to spook his father.

Patience, Perrin.

Oslo nodded. He pushed back his chair with a loud scrape across the scarred linoleum floor. He went to the cabinet over the fridge where Perrin knew he kept a bottle of Scotch.

Oslo wasn't a drinker but he took out the bottle, and after retrieving a fresh glass from the cupboard next to the sink poured himself a healthy shot. Perrin noticed Oslo's hands were trembling.

Oslo downed the scotch in one swallow, coughed then turned and faced Perrin. His strong, pale hands gripped the back of his chair. He leaned into it and the frame creaked. His knuckles were white. "I'm the Smile Killer."

Perrin felt excitement well from within for the first time in his life. He was the proud son of Oslo Hollis the famous Smile Killer! The celebrated serial killer who had killed eight women over the past twenty years.

When the victims were discovered, they wore a frozen smile on their faces that the documentary had said the killer placed there by manually manipulating the face after death.

Perrin chuckled every time he thought of the trademark smile. It was as if the prey was glad they were dead because they left the world with a smile on their face. Hilarious!

Now here he was apprenticing in serial murder under the tutelage of his expert father who started his education by instructing him about the rules: no sexual contact with the prey, only take prey that live alone, and only take prey over the age of forty, preferably over fifty.

It was like Oslo often said, "Spinsters lives were worthless."

Perrin agreed. The sooner worthless spinsters were removed to make room for the more worthy in society the better off everyone would be. Theirs was a mission of mercy.

Of course, working up a profile on selected prey took a lot of work, and a lot of patience.

Carefully selecting the prey was first on Oslo's list.

He was very particular, not that Perrin would ever disagree with an expert. Oslo had killed eight of them over the last twenty years and had never been caught. In fact he had never even been questioned.

That was saying a lot. "The dumb ass cops," Oslo said, "They think all serial killers want to be caught!"

Perrin was forced to agree with his father's practical logic.

How stupid were these cops? After all, how was he supposed to complete his mission if he was in jail?

The Apprentice

Obviously, the cops had watched too much television, or they believed in those mythic profilers. What a lot of nonsense.

Their motto was; so many to remove and so little time.

Perrin accompanied Oslo on visits to shopping malls and banks and even the airport hunting for potential targets.

Homeless prey were no good, they didn't have homes were they could work without risk of detection.

And just because the prey was at a bank or at the airport by themselves, even if they were in the right age range, didn't mean they were a perfect target. It seemed there were an awful lot of widows in the world.

"Look for wedding rings," Oslo instructed him.

Prey that was too wealthy was also no good. They often had drivers, bankers, or lawyers that would miss them. They weren't thieves so who cared how much money the prey had or didn't have. Only the mission was important.

If the cops found the prey too quickly it was a problem.

"Forensics," Oslo said, "the more rotted they were the harder it was for the forensic experts to find the minuet evidence they strained from the prey."

Spinsters had certain habits. They kept their bankbooks in their purses until they were asked for them at the teller. They wore clothes that, while they weren't shabby, weren't new either, and they were not what the beautiful people called attractive.

Usually they were in a hurry to get back to their small dog or pussycat. Oslo told him to listen for the prey to mutter something to themselves about their beloved pets. Concern over pets was a sure indicator the prey lived alone.

Widows were also no good because they often had children who checked on them. This could be messy and would result in the prey's discovery far too soon.

No. A good old-fashioned rotting corpse slowly beginning to smell as it ripened in the warm summer air, now that was a good kill.

Perrin warmed at the thought of the prey he was about to personally kill bleeding out then gasping its last breath as he stared at the prey hog tied on the bed. Its eyes were open, unfocussed, and sleepy. Gradually its eyesight must have cleared because its gray-green eyes popped wide with terror.

Good. Perrin grinned and raised his index finger to his lips as the prey began to protest in a low mumble behind the strip of duct tape covering its mouth.

It stopped and began to struggle against the rope securing its wrists and ankles. Fear and puzzlement swept over the pale skin of its face.

Perrin felt a thrill run through him as he stared at it. This experience was better than he had ever imagined it could be.

"Come here," said Oslo.

Perrin looked up to see his father standing at the foot of the bed, his bulky form silhouetted by the single side table lamp resting on top of a four drawer dresser against the wall behind him. It was the only light in the room. Perrin had made sure only one light was lighted in the tiny apartment bedroom.

Oslo said, "Minimal light made the setting eerie and terrifying for the prey."

Perrin had been resting on his hands bracketing the prey as he hovered over the struggling form lying on its back beneath him.

He pushed upward with his hands until his slight frame was off the bed. He pulled his black knit shirt down with both glove-encased hands as he stood up. He walked to the end of the bed to stand beside his father.

"You do it," gasped Oslo his breathing heavy. Perrin was surprised his father was breathing so hard. Surely, they hadn't worked that hard…so far.

In Oslo's right hand was a long-bladed, razor-sharp Bowie knife. Perrin knew it was heavy, very heavy.

Oslo kept the knife in the bottom of his toolbox wrapped in a worn piece of brown oil-stained leather. He told Perrin the weathered leather strip was from a vest worn by Buffalo Bill, but somehow Perrin doubted it.

He scanned the struggling prey dressed in her ankle-length cotton nighty. He felt the power that was his for the taking. It coursed through his veins. He was life and death. Life was his to give and his to take.

Lois Kildair. Spinster. Age sixty-three. Retired librarian. Three cats and a budgie in a gilded cage. Perfect. The perfect prey.

Perrin accepted the knife from Oslo and smiled as he gripped the heavy handle. The weight felt good in his hand. He moved toward the struggling prey.

***

Suzie White looked up from her computer screen where she had very nearly completed her report when Ozzie Wilson sat down heavily in his desk across from hers.

Ozzie was the old hand in their partnership. He'd been a homicide detective for fifteen years. She'd only made detective five years ago.

Three of years of that she worked burglary, until she was reassigned to homicide. Her dream job.

Ozzie was a large man who loved his donuts. She swore his pores oozed sugar and fat. He was sweating profusely when he sat down with a heavy sigh.

"Well?" asked Suzie her thin eyebrows high on her dusky forehead.

Ozzie may have an ample paunch hanging over his belt, and he might not be the best dresser in the room, but he had a sharp mind and good instincts. He was a good cop and she was glad when she was partnered with the Oz.

He looked over at her and smirked. "I think the kid's involved. I don't know how…yet."

Suzie's lips smiled but her eyes were deadpan. "The DA said we have to leave it alone. He's glad we got the Smile Killer."

Ozzie leaned back in his chair and chuckled coldly. "Yeah. Right. The guy had a heart attack while the boy was slicing and dicing the librarian with a Bowie knife." He shook his head as his expression became sad. "We didn't get anyone. Truth is Oslo Hollis dropped dead in our laps."

"What did the DA say was gonna happen to the kid we found at Kildair's place?"

Ozzie frowned and his bravado evaporated. "He's being locked up in the nut house up in Cherryville. And he'll be gettin' out some day…."

Suzie shook her head. "Yeah…it's hard to imagine. Only fifteen and he thought this guy Hollis was his father. Said he was Hollis' apprentice. I checked on him —"

She read from her report; "Perrin Dystry: parents, Fered and Carmella Dystry killed in a car crash in '96.

"As far as we can tell ever since then the kids pinballed his way through the foster home system. Now he's gonna live in a nut house for a few years." She shook her head. "He sure freaked when the paramedics told him Hollis had croaked. Good thing the black and white arrived right after the ambulance or we'd have two paramedics bodies to clean up."

Ozzie nodded. He crossed his feet on top of his desk and locked his meaty fingers behind his head then leaned back. "Yeah, kids can be so easily mixed up by bad parentental figures."

Yeah, thought Suzie as she turned back to study the photo of the kid in the file. Especially when he thinks his father is training him in the serial killer apprenticeship program.

The Apprentice

On days like these she wondered if maybe she should have stayed in burglary division. She snapped the folder shut and dropped it in the to-be-filed bin on her desk on top of all the others.

She sighed. The captain had assigned them a fresh case half an hour ago.

On to the next case.

A Beautiful Friendship

THE AIR REEKED WITH the thick smell of oil and gasoline. The noxious, sickening fumes mingled with a hint of burnt gunpowder. The smells invaded Chase Valentine's nose leaving a vaguely metallic taste in her mouth.

Crouched uncomfortably behind a rusting steel drum she licked her cracked, dry lips. The mounting tension and the too-dry air had affected her more than she thought it would.

Rising slowly from her haunches, her muscles protesting every inch, she peered over the top of the drum into the inky darkness.

The loading dock was littered with oil drums, any one of which could be hiding an enemy or her target. Oscar Montoya had to be hiding in here somewhere.

And she was going to have to find him.

Problem was Oscar was armed to the teeth. Odd how disgraced millionaires who hire beautiful private investigators object to being brought to justice when things go bad.

Releasing her cell phone from the holster on her hip, she flipped it open. The small LCD screen lit up, just the phone beeped loudly in the silence.

She cursed under her breath as the words low battery flashed repeatedly across the screen. "If only there's time —"

Her long fingers flashed across the illuminated keypad, 9-1-. Her fingers hung frozen over the remaining one when the screen changed to Have a Nice Day then went dark. A disheartened sigh escaped between her lips. "Sorry, baby. I didn't have time to charge you."

The call informing her Montoya was hiding here arrived just as she arrived home form a stake out. She didn't have time to recharge it before she had to race to the warehouse. Her usual luck had failed her this time.

Placing the dead phone back in its holster she cursed herself again. Her ragged breath echoed in her ears. At least Oscar had stopped shooting.

Somewhere to her right in the darkness was, Rex

Harper, her newly acquired partner. Not that she needed a partner, but Oscar had hired them both without them knowing about the other, until ten minutes ago. Oscar obviously thought he'd play one against the other.

She gritted her teeth and a smirk played across her lips. Wrong again, boyo.

The cool handle of her Dad's 9mm Glock felt comfortable in her hand. When she'd inherited The Valentine Detective Agency after her father's death she'd assumed all his tools of his trade, including the reliable Glock.

Where the hell was Rex?

In the darkness, she skirted the field of oil drums then, keeping her head low, scurried like a spider pressing her back against a brick wall to her right and behind her. Always keep something between you and any possible enemies behind you, her dad used to tell her.

The bricks felt solid against her leather jacketed back. Her heart thumped in her chest. She willed herself to remain calm, but kept the Glock at the ready.

A sharp scrape that sounded as if it were almost beside her brought her internal sensors to full alert. Chase froze where she stood her breathing now rapid in her ears.

She strained her hearing to catch any additional

sounds.

A throaty voice whispered her name causing her heart leap into her throat and her index finger to tighten on the guns trigger. "Chase, it's me —"

"By God," she replied, her whispered words clipped with tension. "Damn it, Rex, I could have shot you —"

"But you didn't," said Rex with a hint of sarcasm in his tone.

The man was incorrigible, but that face...oo la la. With ice blue bedroom eyes, and wavy dark-brown hair Rexy boy he was just too handsome for his own good.

"Do you think we should get a cup of coffee after this case is over?" She heard Rex's deep voice coming from her immediate left. He was close. Too close.

Somehow, in the darkness, he'd managed to sneak up beside her without her realizing it. She chastised herself. This wasn't a good thing to happen to a detective. Dad would be disappointed. She determined she would do better in the future. But for right now....

"How can you be so calm?" she whispered.

"My cell phone is fully charged..." he paused then added, "I keep a spare with me when I'm on a case. And an extra suit of clothes in my car trunk. You never know when you'll need 'em."

Chase wondered why she hadn't thought of such

obvious things. After all detective work meant long hours. It wasn't a nine-to-five job. She had a lot learn. If only dad were here.

Her thoughts were interrupted when the dead calm air was torn violently by the sudden appearance of a roaring helicopter that flew low over the steel corrugated storage sheds littering the docks visible form where they were hiding on the loading dock. A brilliant spotlight affixed to its belly forced Chase to squeeze her eyes shut. Her long blonde hair whipped about her head in the suddenly churned, rough air.

She raised her hands to shield herself from the violent down draft caused by the helicopters rotors. She opened one eye to see Rex signalling to the occupants with his snub-nosed .38. Rex was a cliché. Nobody carried snub-nosed .38's anymore. Who did he think he was Joe Friday?

He motioned to the sheds in the distance. That's where the most recent shots had come from.

When the helicopter disappeared from overhead headed for the sheds beyond her dishevelled hair settled around her shoulders once more. Chase was certain her hair must look as if she'd combed it with an eggbeater. Which in a manner of speaking was accurate.

The helicopters white spotlight speared the

dock in a roving pattern hovering over the sheds and eight-foot high stacks of oil barrels searching like a bloodhound hot on the trail of its prey.

Finally, it settled into a hover like any good bird dog would do and pointed the nose of the aircraft downward its beam of white light bathing a row of three-high stacked steel drums.

Rex glanced at her with an easy casual smile splitting his handsome features. He pulled back his navy blue windbreaker revealing a trim torso and slipped his gun into the shoulder holster beneath the thin nylon jacket. "Well, I guess the cops are gonna take care of 'ol Oscar."

Just as he spoke three black and whites, no doubt filled with officers of the cities finest, came screaming onto the dock their red, blue, and white rollers flickering off the sheds. The three squad cars headed straight for the target painted by the helicopter.

Oscar appeared — his eyes wild and angry stood up from behind the drums with his empty hands held up in surrender.

Chase stared at Rex with a smirk on her lips. "Well, I guess we better get that coffee." She smiled at him and holstered her pistol on her hip.

Rex laughed and placed one muscular arm

around her shoulder. "Ya know, Chase, I love the way you handle yourself. Maybe you and I should go into business together."

Chase nodded and ran one hand though her hair to smooth away the blonde strands that bracketed her face. "Yeah…maybe…"

"After all, you're old man and I did some freelance work together a couple of years back. And I really love what you've done with your hair."

Chase couldn't help but laugh. Rex the charmer. But, Dad worked with Rex? Funny he'd never mentioned it.

She shrugged. Maybe Rex and I would make a good team. She glanced at him then smiled to herself. It felt right.

As Bogart once said, this is the start of a beautiful friendship. And maybe more, much more.

The Parrot of Doom

I HAD NEVER SEEN A REAL PARROT in the flesh (or should I say in the feather), before today.

From where I sat on the worn leatherette sofa in my partner, Morton Edge's, parents recreation room I stared at the brightly colored green, and yellow (but mostly green) parrot, with a mustard yellow stripe across his beak. The bird sat on a perch in a cage that appeared to be designed to hold the Count of Monte Cristo it was so big.

The parrot (Edge explained his name is Hercules) had been dropped off by a client, and we were to interrogate it.

"So what is the parrot supposed to tell us?" I asked.

The Parrot of Doom

Edge looked up from the romance novel he'd been reading, his hazel eyes free from emotion. He rarely displays human emotion because he thinks it's a sign of weakness. I think it shows we're all human. I sometimes wonder if Edge is human because he sees the world in such a different way. Then again this is the reason he's so gifted at deductive reasoning, and so bad at human relations.

Human relations is my job at Razor and Edge Investigations. I'm the one who wears out his shoe leather.

"Razor, please refer to the parrot as Hercules. He understands our every word, and I'm told he's offended when referred to as an object."

Objectifying a bird? Now I really have heard everything.

"Huh, yeah, sorry, Hercules," I said, directing my words to the parrot staring back at me with one coal-black eye.

I almost jumped out of my skin when the parrot spoke. "No worries," he said. "Please call me Hercules."

"Uuuuhhh, yeah, OK." My cheeks grew warm. I couldn't believe it but I was embarrassed. I shifted my bony behind on the sagging sofa cushion. The darned thing is so old and ratty sometimes the springs press the flesh with the occupant.

This old sofa is where the butt meets the road.

I gathered my rattled senses and decided I better speak to the parrot. "So, Hercules, what is it you're supposed to tell us?"

The reply was immediate. He shuffled along the perch farther away from me then said, "About Mr. Cunningham's affair."

Hercules was certainly clear, but I was confused. I'd missed something so I directed my next question to my partner. "Edge, I'm obviously out of the loop, could you perhaps explain what's going on, and why Hercules is here?"

Edge closed his novel, after slipping in a bookmark, then set the book on the end table next to his Barcolounger. "Do you wish to explain, Hercules?"

"After you, Mr. Edge."

Oh, brother. To this day I think Hercules was mocking me.

Edge nodded sagely. "Mrs. Cunningham contacted me asking us to follow her husband because she believed he was being unfaithful. She said she'd pay us any amount we asked for. I explained we do not take those kind of cases."

Though I knew he was right, I was disappointed we'd lost a paying client to a little thing like ethics.

The Parrot of Doom

I frowned and glanced at the parrot sitting serenely on his perch then back at Edge. "If you refused the case then why is the pa—I mean, Hercules, still here?"

"Because he knows something about Mrs. Cunningham's murder."

To say I was shocked by this revelation would be an understatement of the first magnitude. "What? Mrs. Cunningham is dead? So who brought us the bird?"

"Mr. Cunningham," said the parrot.

I paused to consider the information I had so far. Mrs. Cunningham calls us to hire us to follow her husband who she thinks is having an affair. She is then murdered, and her grieving husband brings us the bird. What? This is nuts.

"But why would Mr. Cunningham bring us the bird?"

Edge shook his head. "He didn't," my partner said matter of factly.

"I called Mr. Edge," said Hercules.

I gawked at the parrot. He called Edge?

Edge chuckled. "Sorry, Razor, I've been having too much fun. Please forgive me." He paused and his lips formed a crooked smile. "Hercules knew Mrs. Cunningham had called us and pressed the re-dial on the phone.

He told me that he'd witnessed Mr. Cunningham killing his wife. He was indeed having an affair, and planned to run off with his lover.

"After Hercules called me I contacted Detective Aimes telling him I had spoken to a witness to a murder, and that the murderer was about to kill the witness."

"Too true," interrupted Hercules.

Edge smiled then continued. "I gave Aimes the address and the police arrived in time to catch Mr. Cunningham attempting to flee, and they saved Hercules from certain death."

"I'm the parrot of doom," said Hercules.

Parrot of doom? Oh, brother. who knew a parrot could be so dramatic. Then again it would make a good blog title.

"So back to my original question," I said. "Why is he here?"

"The Cunningham's adult daughter is flying in from Los Angeles tomorrow. She'll take Hercules back with her. We're looking after him until then."

"Oh." I eased back against the sofa cushion.

I snatched the TV remote off the scarred pine coffee table in front of the sofa. "Wanta watch some TV, Edge?"

"I like the Home and Garden Network," said Hercules.

I looked at Edge. "Edge?"

He shrugged. "Parrot's choice."

I turned the television on and changed the channel to the Home and Garden Network.

Parrots choice indeed. Stupid parrot's gonna be doomed alright.

Boomerang

SERENDIPITY.

Life is filled with moments of serendipity.

After all my life's work was as much a surprise to me as anyone. After serving in the first gulf war, I found killing people was my destiny. Being paid large sums of money for doing something you love is the bonus.

Now here I sit in smoky pub of a cockroach-infested hotel on the downtown eastside of Vancouver, sipping a warm beer beside one of the cockroaches. This particular cockroach appears to be the most hard luck thief you have ever met. I'm wondering how I was going to slip away.

Boomerang

I couldn't very well walk out the front door because I had stirred up the cops like an angry hornets nest after I had dotted the "I" of Mrs. Reginald Phillips.

My signature is to shoot the target once in the head — what I call "dotting the I" —with a soft-tipped bullet. This creates maximum splatter as the bullet spreads out after contact and blows a large hole in the back of the skull creating a shower of brain matter and blood. This causes witnesses to react with horror and panic allowing me time to escape. The challenge is you have to get really close to the target.

Mr. Phillips was the Donald Trump of Vancouver; he owned most of the glass and steel monuments-to-better-living that decorated the downtown skyline. The guy must have a net worth of at least a billion bucks.

Unfortunately, for Mrs. Phillips, 'ol Reggie wouldn't cooperate with the nastier elements of the construction industry. While it is not my place to speculate about the reasons for the elimination of a target, I read the newspapers like everyone else.

Two days after a very public dispute with the heads of the construction unions an envelope arrives in my drop box filled with cash and surveillance photos of the target. (My fee is usually twenty thousand dollars. The unnamed client paid me twice my usual fee because this was a high profile job.

It would also allow me to lie low on a foreign beach for an extended luxury holiday.)

At first, I am doubtful I can make this a clean kill and consider refusing the job. I knew 'ol Reggie boy had his own security goons so I'd need to plan this one carefully. After all, I want to get away from it all to enjoy my fee.

I follow the Phillips around town for two months prior to the hit in order to document their every move. Finally, an opportunity presents itself that will be perfect. I decide to make the hit on an upcoming Wednesday.

Frankly even I am surprised when my plan plays out exactly as I envision it.

Reggie and his wife — whose name was Veronica, if I remember correctly, or was her name Victoria? Not that it really matters — will be at the grand opening ribbon cutting ceremony of his new luxury apartment tower. There will be a large crowd comprised of his employees, and local newspaper, radio, and television news people. A perfect crowd of unfamiliar faces I will be mingle with to get in close. I even have a fake press pass to get past security. I love the thrill of a close kill.

Boomerang

My scouting report indicates the egotistical bastard forces his employees to attend his openings to applaud his growing empire and increasing personal wealth. To any of his employees who refuse to attend he gives them their walking papers. Charming...

I plan to disguise myself as an old man. My father was a movie makeup artist. He taught me his craft when I was a teenager with the hope I would eventually join him in the family business. Unfortunately, Dad and Mom died in a car crash just before I left for the gulf.

My disguise work is perfect. Wherever he is, I'm certain Dad's proud of me.

After mingling with the crowd, I get close then, with my homemade silencer affixed to the barrel of my untraceable pistol, I dot Mrs. Phillips "I".

As I anticipated, the resulting pandemonium covers my escape to a nearby alley I selected in advance. It is here I discard my disguise and dispose of the gun in a dumpster then disappear into a pre-selected pub.

So here I am, sitting next to Avi Kumar who reeks of mold. He sat down at my table after I arrived. And he's talking my ear off. I nod my head as if I'm listening to his every word while taking the occasional sip of the warm sleeve of beer that long ago lost its foam cap.

My eyes scrutinize the dimly lit pub from the plain black plastic dust-covered fixtures hanging low over the round terrycloth covered tables to the vacant faces of the working class customers. The place reeks of beer, stale cigarette smoke, and sweat. A real working man's bar. My kind of place.

The bartender is a raven-haired woman with a lean figure. She appears to be no more than thirty-five, but her hard features give her the appearance of a weather beaten sailor. Her emotionless gaze suggests she has fought off one too many drunks in her day. Our waiter's large belly hanging over his belt tells me he has consumed generous quantities of this establishments wares.

My plan is to leave after a couple of hours and take a bus home. For now I am listening to the felonious exploits of a two-time loser.

Avi's dark skin is marred with an angry scar that runs down the right side of his face from beside his right eye to his wide chin. He sports the baggy clothing gangsta look that is the rage in the music videos; his bald head appears oddly shaped like one of those misshapen pumpkins left over after Halloween.

Avi's not the master criminal type. He tells me he held up a laundry mat on his last job. He did two years less a day for the big soiled diapers caper.

Boomerang

I am surprised he is telling me any of this crap. I might be a cop for all he knows.

Yeah, the guys a real super villain. Where is Superman when you need him?

It was a good thing I had dropped my .32 caliber Ruger in the dumpster in the alley two blocks away. If I still had my gun I would definitely have a hard time resisting the urge to dot this guys "I" free.

"I have a great job planned and I need a partner… you wanta come with me?" says Avi his words slurred from the two beers he has inhaled since he sat down.

I am about to refuse this excellent career opportunity when I see a gaggle of uniformed cops accompanied by two plain-clothes men, who have to be Phillips security linebackers, come through the twin oak doors that led to the sidewalk. A cloud of steam follows them in and I smell the rain that has started to fall outside.

It's time to leave.

"Sure, Avi I'd be happy to," I say sounding cheery. For a second I think I may be laying it on a little thick, but my doubts are quickly erased when a sloppy smile crosses Avi's face and he grunts. "I gotta a car parked nearby," he says.

I slap him on the shoulder. His faded blue jean jacket is soft under my touch.

"Great. Why don't you and I talk about the job on the way?" I indicate the uniforms making their way through the pub. They stop occasionally asking for identification from patrons at random. The low murmur of conversation masks the questions-asked-and-answers- given. The place is packed for a Wednesday night, but since we're far enough back in the gloom, they don't notice us yet. Unfortunately this won't last long.

Avi glances at the cops and nods. "I hate pigs," he mutters.

He and I stand as one and head for the rear door that leads to the alley. Once outside I consider breaking his neck and leaving him. But since I am no longer in disguise, and since the waiter that served us has seen us together, I decide to wait.

We make it to his car, a rusting late model Chevy, and I offer to drive. Given his unsteady feet the cops'd stop him if he drove. I think 'ol Avi has had a snoot full before he got to the pub.

As we drive on the rain-slicked streets, he instructs me to head for Southwest Marine Drive. Avi says a new Happy-Mart has opened in that area. He tells me his second cousin went to high school with the night manager, a fat wimp named Albert.

Boomerang

Fat Albert is going to be taking the afternoon bank deposit to the bank an hour from now at ten o'clock. His plan is to jump Albert and steal the deposit.

I want to strangle this moron. Hasn't he ever heard of debit cards, credit cards, and checks?

He grins and says, "I know what your thinking… there won't be a lot of cash, right?" I nod but keep my eyes on the road, and the speedometer so I don't drive too fast. We don't need to attract unwanted attention from some eager cop.

He laughs, his arm resting across the back of the bench seat of his ancient Chevy, and says, "My cousin says half of their daily take is cash and they do twenty thousand per shift."

Ten thousand? Cash? Hmmm…if it's true then I will be able to extend my holiday. I glance at Avi and wonder about the shape of the splatter pattern his misshapen head will make when I blow a hole through his head. No one is gonna miss this guy.

"You help me with the job and I'll cut you in for twenty-five percent."

"A quarter share? That's all?" I try to sound indignant because I know I am going to get a one hundred percent share.

He laughs again. "My cousin gets twenty-five and you get twenty-five. I get half because…." he pats his jacket …" I have the gun."

**

We arrive with half an hour to spare. I get us some coffee in Styrofoam cups from a nearby 7-11 and we sit in the parking lot waiting for Albert. Finally, when my patience is waning, he appears.

Albert is wearing a white dress shirt and navy windbreaker and black rimmed glasses, and yes, he is a very fat man. Beads of sweat dot his wide pale forehead. Tucked under his right arm is a brown bank deposit bag.

Avi and I get out of the Chevy and walk toward Albert who is concentrating on fishing in his windbreaker pocket for his car keys. He is standing beside a late model steel gray Toyota Corolla.

My temporary partner in crime moves behind the fat man and pulls out a pistol, which he sticks it in Albert's back. For his part Albert looks like he's about to have a heart attack he's bathed in sweat and trembling. I detect the odor of urine. Great. The fat boy's bladder has let go.

"Move and I'll kill you," says Avi. He says it with sufficient menace I even believe he might kill the poor guy.

Boomerang

I step up and yank the deposit envelope out of Albert's pudgy outstretched hand. I glance at Avi who has a sneering grin on his face and nod.

We turn and start back for the Chevy.

"Hold it!" says a voice behind us. I freeze while Avi turns the gun held level in his right hand. With distain evident in his voice Avi says, "It's okay. It's only Albert."

I turn around to see Albert is holding a snub-nosed revolver in trembling hands. He looks like he's going to shake the thing apart. Is he serious? He's going to get himself killed.

I decided I had better stop this thing before it gets messy. "Com'on, Albert. Drop the gun or …" I indicate my partner, "… he'll shoot you. Do you want to die for the Happy-Mart deposit?"

Albert's eyes are wide with his face contorting with inner confusion. "Do you guys know me? Do I know you?"

The air erupts with a gunshot. Albert's white shirt explodes with a flood of red and he drops to his knees the gun leaving his hand to clatter sharply across the pavement. The now very dead Albert falls on his face with a soggy smack.

I look at Avi as if to ask him why he shot fat Albert. He shrugs. I don't care either.

Happy-Mart will find another night manager.

"I guess we better get another car," he says. I realize the Chevy wasn't really his car. Interesting, the guy really did have an actual plan. I gain a new respect for my temporary partner.

I nod in concurrence. After scanning the parking lot for cars that are easy to steal, I spot a blue Ford Taurus with a plastic cross hanging from the rear view mirror that will fit the bill nicely.

We head for the car. We break in easily with a lock pick Avi's carrying. He bends down to get underneath the steering and commences to hot-wire it like a pro. Hmmmm…the guy really does have some marketable skills. Too bad he's going to be dead sooner than later

That is when Avi makes his last mistake. He hands me the gun while he arranges the wires. When the car engine starts, he raises his head and I raise the gun and point it at my soon-to-be-late partner. His dark eyes stare at me quizzically.

"You know one thing that bothers me," I ask, "why haven't you asked me my name?"

He smirks. "I know who you are. I don't need your name."

I love the smell of burnt gunpowder.

Boomerang

The pistol jerks in my hand and the back of Avi's head explodes; a shower of blood and brain matter covers the driver's side window behind him. After smacking the window his head slumps forward his chin resting on his chest.

Odd…the bullet should have gone through his skull and shattered the window. I hold the pistol up in the dim light coming from the street and notice the serial number is filed off. My heart freezes. The .32 Ruger … with my fingerprints all over it. My specially made soft tipped bullets would not be able to penetrate the window

I feel the urge to laugh aloud at the irony, wouldn't the cops love to get their hands on this weapon. The gun used to kill three other people tonight has my fingerprints all over it: Mrs. Phillips, a fat Happy-Mart night manager, and the late Avi Kumar, super criminal. Avi must have found my gun in the dumpster before coming into the pub. No doubt a happy coincidence for him.

The Taurus' engine suddenly dies and a voice comes from the car radio. "Don't move. This is the police. You've stolen a bait car. The doors are locked. You cannot escape."

I stare at the boomerang Ruger. Once the cops test the gun and find out where it was used tonight ….

Serendipity. I wonder how Avi knew who I was? And I wonder if life has more surprises in store for me. I raise the pistol to my temple. My only hope is there is a beach on the other side …

Cape Disappointment

1

HANDS TREMBLING, Ben Harris, re-opened the manila file folder lying on his cigarette scarred oak desk in the squad room.

He'd been afraid to open it since the Captain dropped it on his desk, six hours ago. The other six homicide detectives were gone for the day, their stale fast food containers still filling the room with greasy fried odors mingling with the already dusty atmosphere of the squad room.

He was alone.

The patter of rain striking the single paned windows echoed in the quiet of the room competing with his rapidly beating heart. The metal accordion lamp sitting in front of him, near the edge of the desk, cast a yellow pool of light over Kelly Harris' dead eyes staring back at him from the autopsy photo.

Her chalky pallor, blue lips, and battered face failed to reveal the woman who he loved in a previous life. No one knew the bitch the way he did. No one could.

Her body had been fished out of the near freezing water that morning near Cape Disappointment, where she'd been dumped by her killer.

The report said she had not been dead prior to being placed in the gray waters of the rock strewn bay. The coroners' report, in the folder opposite the photo, made it clear she didn't die of hypothermia.

The rocks, with their sharp edges and unyielding steadfastness, had punished her face almost beyond recognition. Looking at the photo he would've recognized her anywhere.

He recalled her full hips and ample bosom laying next to him in bed. And her soft hands caressing his back as they slept curled next to each other in a fetal hug, protected and warm. A lot of time had passed.

His dark navy suit pants rustled softly as with his right hand, he attempted to snap off the lamp switch. His hand shook so violently he had to use the ebony fingers of his left hand to steady himself and take in a few deep breaths. After placing the file folder back on the green blotter covering the burn marks on his desk the trembling finally stopped.

After pausing a few seconds to regain his focus, he managed to push the red slider across the switch assembly thereby interrupting the connection. The white forty-watt bulb dimmed, then went out. Only the remaining heat from the blub served as reminder it had it had been on. That too would soon disappear.

He rose from the ancient tan oak chair, its crushed burgundy cushion doing little to protect his growing secretarial spread. He pulled his matching suit jacket off the chair back. Once the jacket covered his sweat stained white shirt he loosened his red striped power tie around his thick neck and sighed. A deep weariness had invaded his bones. He was so tired.

Wind swept raindrops struck the windows covered with chicken wire mesh in sufficient force to remind him of a war zone. In his youth he'd fought wars not crime.

He picked up the manila folder then walked toward the wood framed glass door leading to the hallway and the old Otis elevators beyond. what little light there was coming through the fogged glass acted as a beacon allowing him to find his way through the darkened room.

Near the door there stood a large shredder over which, fixed to the wall, was a black sign, with large white print.

It read: No investigative files must leave the squad room. All top secret files must be shredded.

Underneath some joker, probably his partner, Miller, had stuck a yellow post-it note with the words, Investigative files are secret files. The "are" was underlined.

Ben smirked as he placed the file in the shredders feeder and hit the green button on the side. The machine sprang to life with a roar filling every wall of the quiet room then quickly consumed the file contents and all.

He snapped the shredders button to the off position and the room returned to a quiet calm.

No one would be investigating this case. Kelly's gone, plain and simple.

The glass in the door rattles as he opened it. He glanced down at the thin strips of paper in the bin beneath the feeder and realized she wasn't worth it. No one was.

The door closed behind him and his footsteps faded into the distance.

2

Rose Thomas studied the dancing snow flakes through the small window of the lumbering 747 as it neared the end of the runway. The city spread out below her lay under a blanket of white. The streets and byways cut black lines like squares on some fairy tale giant's blanket. It felt good to return to Vancouver.

She clipped the fine tipped ball point pen's plastic clip into the rings that ran up the spine of the blue cardboard-protected, ninety-eight cent binder resting open on her lap.

She glanced down at the numbered, finely-etched script on the nine by seven paper with a sense of satisfaction. Her list was ready. Now she was eager to get started.

Jack, her husband of ten years, seated in the seat beside her, was certainly useless when it came to decision making. Her role in life was to be the decision maker in their family. She wore the metaphorical pants.

She smiled to herself as it occurred to her how long she'd been away. New husband, new job, all had changed in the intervening years. She relished the thought of catching up with her old friends, Liz and Carla.

Cape Disappointment

She looked at Jack with his hands gripping the seat rests with an intensity so strong he might break off the arms any second. He may be a coward, but he was her coward and that's what counted. She could keep any man under her thumb, not like some women she knew.

Naturally, she hadn't given him any say in making this trip, even though it was taking time away from her writing, and drained much needed funds from their bank account. A small town cop's salary didn't go far these days. He would just have to work some over time.

Her royalty checks went into her private account, to cover off her writing expenses. Not that they payments were that much, but after this convention that would change.

She'd long considered it odd that her publisher never sent her on book tours. Her first poetry anthology went to print during her college days, some twenty years previous. The book sold well, and finally her second book of Poems was about to be published. Friends who read her work assured her she was a damn good poet.

"You okay, Jack?" He wasn't.

The sweat reeled in sheets off his forehead, and his normally pale face was flushed and blotchy.

Through eyes squeezed tight, like he was being treated to a dance on hot coals, he nodded and said nothing.

She knew he hated flying in any kind of plane, big or small. But then he had always been a baby about such things. Good thing she was here to look after him.

Initially, when she'd told him she was going to Vancouver for the convention, his fear had evaporated until it dawned on him he'd have to fly to get there. His initial reaction was like that of a lap dog, its tail wagging furiously, begging her to take him along for the ride.

As he'd explained, his blue eyes sparkling with delight, he hadn't been to Vancouver in years. In fact, he'd only been here during one cross country road trip with his family when he was ten. Reluctantly, she agreed to let him come with her.

The plane's tires squealed as they came into contact with etched surface of the runway. The sound echoed through the skin of the aircraft. The plane swayed slightly from side to side as it settled nose first then began its roll out. Rose was certain Jack would scream if the movement from side to side continued.

The four turbo fan jet engines attached to the football field sized wings roared in the cabin as the pilot changed the levers to the reverse thruster position.

Cape Disappointment

Simultaneously they were pressed back into their seats as the pilot stepped hard on the brakes in order to impede their forward momentum. Rose felt the tension ease in her husband as the plane began to slow.

Rose could see the flaps were now fully extended out the small, port hole sized window, next to her.

Jack sighed as the single breath he'd been struggling with for the past several minutes, escaped between his dry lips. Sweat stained his yellow golf shirt, and his short, dark hair, normally combed neatly into place, laid pasted flat against his forehead.

Rose reached into her shiny black, plastic coated, purse on the floor underneath the seat in front of her extracted a wad of white tissues and handed them to him.

The plane continued on its drive to the terminal bouncing and shuddered its way across the runaway.

Jack grinned at her, obviously relived at being on sacred ground again. He mouthed a thank you, as he mopped the excess moisture from his head and neck.

She acknowledged him with a regal tip of her head, though her thin lips remained pursed, as if she were a school marm acknowledging her student.

The co-pilots voice echoed over the speaker system welcoming them to their destination, and to issue the usual de-boarding instructions to the passengers.

They were to get off on gate 23 then proceed to the baggage area where their luggage would be unloaded on carousel 23A. Ellen made a quick mental note of this information then looked about her to make sure she had every thing. Yes, her check list was complete.

The plane stopped and everyone around them started standing to open the over head bins and retrieve their valuables. They pushed over one another to drag down their particular bag or jacket from the bin. The petite oriental lady next to her prattled on in Chinese to the lady across the aisle, they were obviously traveling together, though neither of them had said anything to each other for the entire flight.

Jack and Rose were located in the center and window seats, he in the center near the rear of the cabin, so they would be among the last off. Rose decided to wait calmly for their turn while Jack began to fidget uncontrollably. In his view the thing was a flying bomb with wings waiting to happen and he couldn't wait to get to safety.

Cape Disappointment

With the rapid fire words of the little Chinese ladies still permeating her nostrils, and the strong smell of garlic, left by the man seated in front of them, she gave the all clear signal to her husband.

Not needing further encouragement, Jack leapt from his seat, like a rabbit in heat, and hurriedly grabbed their black leatherette over night bag, and her lap top case, from the over head compartment.

He wrestled them to the aisle seat as she undid her seat belt. She prided herself by following instructions to the letter.

Always keep your seat belt fastened until the plane comes to a complete stop at the gate.

These were standard instructions after every flight, and pretty clear ones at that. It bothered her sensibilities when other people ignored the rules. Therefore, she made it her life's ambition to follow instructions, just as an example for everyone else. Jack would sometimes insist on gently teasing her about her obsession, but she insisted it was what made her feel complete.

After Jack moved out of her way she shifted across the row of three seats from where she sat moving toward where he'd been standing. Her pudgy fingers grasped the orange and gray cushions of the seat backs in front of her to steady herself.

Her gray, low rise loafers, with the rubberized soles and simulated leather uppers, made a soft shushing sound on the pale blue carpet of the plane's deck as she moved.

A person of her size was physically challenged by the cabin configuration most airlines insisted upon, which often made getting out of these narrow seats difficult, but not impossible. She longed for them to wake to her disadvantaged group.

Corporate thinking, not customer comfort, paid the bills something she could readily identify with, but was still miffed about.

Jack stepped back as Rose stepped into the aisle and ran her bloated hands down the sides of her forest green pant suit in a losing attempt to smooth out five hours worth of wrinkles. Jack, who was obviously feeling a lot better, grinned at her in his lop sided way.

"We made it," he said.

"Jack, do you always have state the obvious? Pleeease…" She rolled her eyes, then stepped past him headed for the front of the cabin. She could feel the heat of his eyes on her as she walked away, but she knew he'd never say anything about more it.

3

Kelly tied the clean white apron over her pale peach colored uniform, then pushed the stray strands of sandy brown hair behind her right ear. Stray hairs had again broken loose from the hair pins. She took a deep breath, just as she did everyday, then walked out of the combination change room, women's washroom into the staff common area in the back of Willie's Family Restaurant.

Her plain white nurse's shoes made a soft shuffling sound on the burgundy tinted cement floor as she hurried down the corridor.

She passed the dishwashers work area where a new guy, whose name escaped her, was sliding a plastic tray full of dirty plates standing on their edges like a row of soiled wheat into the automatic dishwasher. The rattle of the plates echoed through the confined space of the common area as he forced them inside then, using the handle on the side, brought down the aluminum walls of the cover around them and pushed the large green start button attached to polished solid steel work counter between them.

The array of chemical smells mingled with food smells of all descriptions in this area of the restaurant. This rarely made the dishwasher a popular guy.

She felt her skin crawl as the latest unshaven loser winked at her as she passed by. With a cigarette dangling from between chapped lips, and the greasy shoulder length trails of hair resting on his narrow shoulders, he wasn't the worst horror that Armstrong had hired. At least he didn't make the effort to comb some of those slick strands over the top of the large bald spot on top of his head like the last one.

Along the opposite wall from the dishwasher's station was a row consisting of six shiny steel fridge doors, each the dimension of the average sized man.

She recalled her revulsion when she had first thought about the fact you could store a six-footer in one if you needed to, and not even have to break the legs, as she'd heard morticians sometimes did with dead bodies to get them to fit in standard sized coffins.

She could see Mr. Armstrong, surrounded on two of the four walls of his small six by five workspace, sitting in his office, his smooth hairless scalp titled forward as he concentrated on the documents in front of him.

She tapped lightly on the hollow wood door, once. No answer. Twice. Finally he spoke up.

"Yeah. What the hell is it?" he said, the annoyance evident in his voice.

Cape Disappointment

He pressed forward into the desk as she, barely missing his wheeled chair, swung the door open to his cramped office. She secretly enjoyed making him have to press into his desk with his ever-growing girth making it more difficult with each passing week. Soon he'd not only get a red line across his belly, due to the force he'd use to avoid being hit by the door, but he'd get the door up his ass. Little pleasures, you took them where you could get them. This was a gift.

A deep furrowed brow and angry brown eyes greeted her. When he saw it was Kelly his face changed to a sunny expression, and his yellowed teeth showed from beneath his thick, dark moustache.

It was one of those bushy kinds of moustaches' she'd didn't think anyone had worn since the seventies.

With his wide, soup-stained tie, and the polyester navy pants he wore every day to complete his ensemble, he looked like a throw back in time. Given his attitude toward women, was not such a stretch.

"Kelly, what a nice surprise. I didn't think you'd be on shift today."

"Huh, I'm not actually scheduled to work today, sir. I switched with Alice. I need the money."

She kept her eyes focused on his desk so she didn't have to look directly at him.

She didn't want to risk catching his eye thereby running the risk of forcing the wrong idea into his psyche. The last thing she wanted was him to think was that she was interested, which she most certainly was not.

There were unsubstantiated stories circulating about Mr. Armstrong, and she wasn't about to take any chances they might be true.

When the door opened a momentary look of dismay crossed his face, then changed to what he must've thought was a reasonable facsimile of Romeo.

In his fucking dreams.

"Yeah, I guess that would be alright."

Kelly nodded then closed the door. She smiled to herself as she walked away. Changing shifts with someone was against the rules, and one she'd just broken and gotten away with.

Armstrong's door suddenly flung open and he stuck his head out. "I'll be out later, if anyone comes looking for me." She nodded, knowing she had dodged the bullet.

Feeling lighter inside she walked toward the double hinged door with the glass inset, at eye level, in the center, a feature designed to allow both the waitress' inside and outside to see each other coming.

Cape Disappointment

This little safety item helped avoid collisions, and workers comp claims.

After stepping aside, to allow Kay come through the door gripping, with two hands, a plastic bus tray loaded down with glasses, plates, of various sizes, and cutlery, she entered the customer area of the restaurant ready to take on another day among the living.

4

He slipped away with the intention of leaving Rose to enjoy her four to six afternoon nap in privacy.

Jack gingerly began to ease the door closed, using the burnished gray metal handle, to suite 1407 until, with a sharp click the latch caught. The Astoria Hotel is the finest of moderately priced flop houses in the center of town. Through the heavy pine door he could hear her regular, loud snoring that rattled the strongest of windows. She'd be asleep for a while yet.

He turned and started down the dimly lit hallway, which snaked around a corner out of his field of vision. The pot lights over head created a trail of spots like bread crumbs along the plush ruby and indigo carpet.

He cringed at the sight of then flowery wall paper which lined the walls. The blue, pink and yellow daisies were the gaudiest thing he'd ever seen. Naturally, Rose liked it.

He followed the path laid before him until he returned to the bank of elevators from earlier when he'd carried their luggage from the lobby.

One pot light flickered as he passed like some seventies discotheque lighting system resurrected from obscurity just for him.

It made him think about Kelly and how she'd looked back then, before he'd left to become a cop in Toronto. Those were good days. Fun days.

The urge to dance, screw, and snort anything that was placed before him had given way to responsibility. Rose had made sure of that. She was organized and made his life easier every day.

He stepped into the elevator car and found himself alone, facing a perfect picture of himself. He pressed the lobby button and the doors slid shut with a resounding thump as they made contact. The car began to move.

He gazed at the middle aged man with the receding hairline in front of him. The belly was a little softer and his rugged physique of twenty years ago was just a memory.

He held his breath and pulled his paunchy stomach in just as the bell, indicating the elevator was stopping to load passengers, sounded. The cars jerked to a halt and, after a momentary pause, which provided him the opportunity to let out his breath. He stuck his hands in his pockets in an attempt to appear casual. He didn't feel casual, he felt uncomfortable. he hadn't been to a bar in twenty years.

A young, well-scrubbed couple nicely dressed couple entered the elevator car.

The doors then closed once more and the elevator continued its downward journey. The glowing row of numbers over the doors inside the car lit up then went dark as they passed each floor on their way to the L. The lobby.

Why is this thing taking so long?

To pass the time, Jack studied the couple.

She was blonde, with the California thing happening. She wore wearing a blue and red striped tee shirt accompanied by tan slacks neatly pressed. The fresh razor sharp creases ran down both slim legs ending at the shiny knee-high heels showing from beneath the cuffs.

The guy, looking like a Back Street Boy. He had on a jet black tee shirt with the arms ripped off to the shoulder, and dark blue jeans. On his feet he wore white Nike's.

They each had an arm wrapped around the other, and were solely focused on gazing longingly into the each others eyes, ignoring him as if he was on another planet.

He concluded they were newlyweds. "Honeymoon?" he said his deep voice resonating off the constricted walls.

Cape Disappointment

The guy, his face changing to one of anger with a speed which startled Jack, removed his arm from the woman's waist then stepped up to within inches of Jack's face. Jack could feel the heat of his breath and smell the steak he'd had for dinner.

"None of your fucking business." He pressed his index finger into Jack's chest, "old man," he added for emphasis.

Jack was tempted to take the guy down, but he restrained himself. The guy was right. It wasn't none of his business. "Sorry." He shrugged keeping his hands inside his trouser pockets.

Before the situation got out of hand the doors opened into the lobby and, after poking Jack's chest once more, again for emphasis, the couple exited the car together leaving him standing there alone. They whisked, like some human tornado, through the lobby then out the glass windmill doors into the street out front.

The man in front at him grunted at him then also entered the lobby disappearing toward the restaurant.

Jack gathered his composure, shook his head, and stepped out of the elevator. He cleared his throat. He'd never been so embarrassed.

He studied the front desk area until he spotted a sign hanging over an archway at one end of the large room. With tan colored wing chairs pressed into every available space. Large bay windows and orange clay pots containing a plethora of flowering indoor plants were scattered everywhere.

He sauntered past the large oak front desk, where a lone male desk clerk with blow dried brown hair. His eyes followed Jack as came toward him.

He was on the phone obviously speaking with a guest who's needs had not been met, evidenced by the pained expression on the clerks face.

Jack smiled and nodded as he went by and the clerk smiled back weakly then continued to explain that what ever the problem was hotel policy.

Jack followed the signs until he found the hotel bar. Once inside he realized immediately it was unusual. The bar itself, a long expensive teak surface surrounded by high backed wicker chairs, had a view, on the wall behind, a swimming pool.

Not the full pool, just the under water portion, so that when sitting at the bar you had a view of the people swimming on the other side of the glass.

From his experience in interrogation rooms he recognized the glass was one sided.

Cape Disappointment

Bar patrons could see in the water, but anyone swimming on the other side couldn't see inside the bar. It was truly unique in his experience.

Behind the bar stood the well groomed bartender. His short wiry curls and pencil thin moustache made him appear more youthful than he probably was. He was standing with his hands behind his back wearing a navy vest, with the hotel logo on one side, a black bow tie, and a perfectly pressed powder blue shirt.

On his face was the most dazzling smile Jack had seen this side of toothpaste commercial. "Hello, sir," he said in a sing song tone. Jack thought the guy must be lonely or something, but he decided to play along.

"Hi, yourself. How about a beer?" Jack climbed aboard one of the wicker chairs to take it for a test drive.

"Certainly, any particular kind?"

"Naw, just whatever you have on tap."

The bar tender nodded then, after pulling down a pilsner glass from the over head rack, he drew a frothy glass of the amber liquid, then placed the glass in front of Jack on a cardboard coaster with the hotel logo stencilled across it.

Jack instinctively reached for his wallet.

"You a hotel guest, sir?"

Jack nodded. "Room 1407."

The bar tender wrote the number down on a slip of paper next to the register. "The charge will appear on your bill at check out time."

"Thanks." The bar tender nodded then turned and walked into the stock room, through a door to the left of the pool window, while Jack sat and stared at the blue water picture window before him fascinated by the mind of the person who'd thought this idea up. There was no one swimming at the moment, but Jack's imagination quickly ran away with him.

Then it struck him, as lightning often does on a clear summer day, hard to imagine on a November day in Vancouver. Kelly. An irresistible urge gripped him to call Kelly.

It had been far too long, and after all, how often would he be in Vancouver?

Stepping away from the bar, his beer half finished, he headed for the nearest pay phone. He was filled with child like excitement as his eyes searched for the familiar symbol on the lobby signs when he remembered Rose sleeping upstairs. She would never approve of him speaking with an old girl friend. He shrugged.

What the hell why not? What would it hurt?

5

Her tired muscles screamed in protest as Kelly stooped to pick up the community paper from the dusty burgundy carpet on the lobby floor of her apartment building. She made the additional effort because she liked to read the local stuff better than the morning tab or the pretentious afternoon edition, which billed itself as the source for news in Vancouver.

Exactly whose source they were supposed to be had always been a mystery to her.

On a sidebar on the cover she noticed there was an advertisement for the Vancouver Writers Convention being held at the Astoria downtown.

Folding the paper under her arm she scanned her copper colored metal mailbox and saw it was empty. For today at least there were no bills coming due, but there soon would be.

She walked to end of the carpeted hallway which muffled her footsteps and climbed there two flights to her apartment.

Once inside she locked the deadbolt and slipped the light chain into place. Her mother warned her that single girls in the big city were often targets of the pervert league.

She doffed her white shoes by the front door, threw the newspaper on the over stuffed worn green couch pushed against the wall of the living room, then padded in her beige nylon'd feet into the kitchen.

The remnants of the beef stew she'd made for dinner for the following week still lingered in the air. The covered stone wear cooking pot sat in the old fifties refrigerator across from the white heavy ceramic sink.

The thing that made these three story walk ups popular was their character. The hardwood floors and expansive windows all around gave them a charm hard to find in this era of glass and concrete.

The answering machine blinked her so, after filling the tea kettle with water and placing it over a gas burner on the white ceramic stove, which she lit with a single turn of the third from the left of the solid black plastic knobs lined up across the front, she pushed the button to listen as she padded toward the bedroom with the intent of changing into her slob wear.

After she'd left the room she heard the machine beep then a voice from her past echoed down the silent hallway.

With her uniform dress bunched around her waist, revealing her black lace bra underneath, she raced back into the kitchen. With trembling hands she again called up the message.

Cape Disappointment

Sure enough there it was him deep, sexy voice and all. Jack's here, in Vancouver, but he didn't say where exactly, he said he'd call her back.

Remembering his wife was a poet she retrieved the paper she'd tossed on the worn green couch when she'd entered and scanned the article about the writer's conference. The Astoria—he was at the Astoria. She looked out side the front window at the light snow falling and realized he was only blocks from where she stood right now. Her hands shook with anticipation.

6

Barney Armstrong watched Kelly walk away then turned back toward his desk. He'd been attempting to get into her pants since the first day he'd laid eyes on her, but so far he'd been unsuccessful. He shrugged and returned to re-read the letter sent to him from Shirley at head office.

The company logo glowed under the fluorescent lights directly over his small cheap laminated desk. It consisted of a gold W with two eagles surrounding it seemingly in worship of their founder, William "Willie" Woodson, a poor dirt farmer who'd gotten lucky.

Well today was Barney's day. His day to get lucky. His day to buy those expensive Italian leather shoes he'd had his eye on at the mall.

He pulled out a plastic red pen from white chipped coffee cup he used as a pen holder and circled the most important paragraph of Shirley's letter.

The letter said she'd would be at the Astoria later this afternoon to discuss terms. If he didn't show the deal would be off. He glanced at the white faced electric clock with the black numbers and the thin hand slowly marching through the minutes and seconds to his future. Things were about to change for Barney Armstrong.

Cape Disappointment

Easing back against the hard cushion of the worn gray secretarial chair he ran his hand over his damp bald head. Glancing up Barney saw Albert, the new dishwasher he'd hired the previous Friday, share his toothless grin as he caught him standing, arms at his side, watching him. The reflective polished surface of the twelve foot steel work table was piled in front of him. Barney scowled at the lazy bastard and raised his right index finger to point at the mountain of soiled work that needed to be scaled within the next hour in preparation for the hungry lunch crowd.

The ex-con, still grinning like a school boy on the last minute of the last day of school before Christmas holidays, chuckled and nodded. Favors to old friends led to a road of sorrows. He shook his head at his own stupidity. Who was being dumb shit?

7

Precisely at six thirty Jack glanced at his Timex only to look up as Rose strode into the hotel restaurant. Her purposeful stride, navy blue pant suit with the starched white shirt showing above the row of black buttons which ran up the center, indicated to him she would all business tonight.

As was her practice her black hand bag, the one with the metal clasp at the top, firmly secured of course, straps were slid down over her thick left wrist. Her expression behind her heavy black framed glasses told him she on one of her missions again tonight.

They'd been at the convention for three days now and she'd managed to piss off just about every editor and publisher in attendance. Of course, he dare not tell her retribution would make his life to now seem like a free ride.

She sat down the in the low backed wicker chair across from him and opened her notebook. He with the intention of limiting their conversation picked up the plastic coated menu and began to scan the pages for his choice of supper.

He'd told her before her nap time that he wanted to go out to eat. The food at the hotel, while it's okay, was beginning to taste a little bland to his pallet.

Cape Disappointment

In Smith Falls he enjoyed the hunt for new, more exotic meals while on his meal breaks during patrol shifts. The restaurants in the surrounding communities had a wide range of foods he enjoyed. Japanese, Chinese, Greek, Italian all were available if you knew where to look. Rose had been raised in a British home where meat and potatoes were the staple of the diet. As usual his wishes were vetoed.

Rose checked off something in her book with her red felt tip pen as the waitress, a red haired woman, heavy around the hips, who wore too much red lip stick and with her face coated in a thick layer of white powder and orange rouge designed to highlight her low cheek bones, made her appear clownish which he didn't think was the look she hoping to achieve. This coupled with the lingering stench of cigarettes, which he'd unfortunately discovered when she'd recorded his drink order approached their table.

She must've sensed his discomfort earlier because her odor had changed and she now smelled of enough perfume to be employed in a French whorehouse mingled with the cigarettes it was an unpleasant combination.

Jack had to agree with Rose who wrinkled her nose as they woman approached.

"I'll have a glass of white wine," she said before the waitress could speak. "Chardonnay, not too dry." She cast her gaze on Jack who raised his glass of cheap blended Scotch to show her he already had his.

Rose smiled thinly then picked up her menu. The waitress nodded and started to walk away.

"We'll both have the broiled chicken, no potatoes, with extra vegetables. And make sure the cook knows that the vegetables were over cooked last night." Jack closed his menu and placed it on the table next to him. He didn't want chicken, but what choice did he have? None as usual.

"Yes, of course, ma'am." She gathered their menus then moved away, her pink polyester slacks rubbing furiously, before she became trapped by Rose's fastidious habits.

Little did Rose suspect the waitresses had taken to flipping coins to see who served the woman who needed the attitude adjustment. Tonight this waitress lost the toss.

Rose eased her body against the back of chair. Jack noticed it creaked slightly from the unwanted stress. He caught himself wanting to chuckle at the mental image on Rose toppling to the floor as the chair back broke from the strain. Instead he smiled, his unpolished coffee stained teeth providing his cover.

Cape Disappointment

He glanced at the face of his watch again and saw it was nearing quarter of seven. Soon. Very soon.

"Going somewhere, dear," said Rose, her eyes cast downward focused on the pure white table cloth as snapped the white cloth napkin, with the finely stitched edges, across her lap with one theatrical flourish.

She then placed her elbows on the table and steeple her fingers in front of slightly bowed head, her dark eyes focused on his over the edge of glasses and waited for his response.

Jack felt his heart sink. She knew. That must be it, she knew. "Of course not, honey." He struggled with the words forcing a light tone into his voice.

She laid her fingers flat on the table, which she then smoothed her fingers moving outward from center toward the edges of the heavy linen tablecloth. "You don't look well. You should have a nap after dinner."

He nodded then they lapsed into silence. Rose slipped her handbag off her left wrist, where until this moment she'd keep it secure from all would be muggers, paranoia was her middle name, then unzipped a pocket on one side where she kept her grooming tools and retrieved a white plastic handled nail file. Carefully she laid the file flat on the table cloth then, after ensuring the gold colored latch was firmly in place returned the purse to her wrist.

He was distracted watching Rose engaged in her grooming ballet. Her way of doing the most mundane of tasks had fascinated him for years.

It suddenly dawned on him he couldn't meet Kelly at their agreed upon place and time. When he had spoken with her on the lobby telephone after reading her message, the thirty-dollar tip to the desk clerk had secured his silence. They agreed they wanted it to be at the place where they had met all those years ago, Mustafa's Sahara Nights.

Unfortunately, the discotheque remained a fond memory of their youth. It ewes for the best and probably where such a place should exist.

It had gone out of business along with the best music of the '70's, as far as he was concerned, back in the early eighties.

The high end tourist flea market that Robson street had become with its designer outlet stores, espresso bars and trendy, here-today-gone-tomorrow restaurants had invaded the once, in his opinion, fun part of the city. No wonder the town had grown a rep for being the navy blue blazer amongst the cities in North America.

Instead, they agreed to meet at the coffee shop on Georgia Street at 7:30.

Cape Disappointment

It would be crowded with late Thursday night shoppers by then, and they would just be two people in a crowd.

Now he'd ruined everything. Kelly would think she'd been stood up just like the old days. The disappointment ate at him in the pit of his stomach.

He winced as Rose, who had taken her nail file out of her purse and started mindlessly humming to the beat of the elevator music coming over the restaurant's sound system. This was going to be a long, long night.

8

Kelly walked along the rain soaked pavement her full figure wrapped in the protection of the rain coat she'd purchased last fall in the men's only clothiers shop. It was black with gray trim and not a particularly attractive cut on a woman, but it was practical and that's what counted. The light snow of the last few days had changed to rain, a good thing, but the wind coming from the North Shore mountains still howled down the web of streets in the downtown core.

It was an easy walk from the bus stop on Burrard Street to the mall. She covered the distance in record time. He would be there waiting and she breathlessly wanted to get there as fast as her legs would carry her.

She arrived at the store at the appointed hour and scanned the street outside. With each passing second the anticipation and longing grew inside her. She heard he was a cop now and doing well. Funny how those things work out.

Finally he came into view his waist wrapped in a long black trench coat and a hat pulled down over his eyes to shield himself from the wind and rain.

They would go for a walk on the beach along the shore in West Van. The park near the lighthouse known as Cape Disappointment.

Cape Disappointment

The park's name was due to the high number of deadly shipwrecks in that area back in the early part of the twentieth century. It would be deserted this time of day.

Her long dreamed of romantic evening with the one person that ever really mattered to her was about to become reality. She'd been with other men since those days, but this guy was special. It had taken over twenty years for her to realize it. Today her life would change. Forever.

9

Jack didn't try to call Kelly again. He'd done enough already, far more than he expected he would. There was never any answer at her apartment, and time was running out. Besides he didn't dare, with Rose watching his every move, expect for the four to six p.m. window when she had her daily nap. She was very precise.

Of course he also didn't have the courage to call Kelly again.

Kelly hadn't called back so he assumed he'd blown it, again, or maybe she'd lost interest, which was the more likely scenario.

Two days left of Rose's convention then he could go home where he belonged so who cared.

The feel of the steering wheel of the Chevy cruiser the town council bought for the department last year would be welcomed in his hands. Once he caught to odor of that new car smell he would be home, grounded for life. The sound of the three hundred and fifty cubic inch engine would course through his butt again.

Ten years to retirement would be his end. And his life with Rose would continue as before.

The red faux leather wing chair squeaked loudly as he shifted his weight to get more comfortable.

Cape Disappointment

The damn things were in reality medieval torture devices for guys like him with bad backs.

Glancing at Rose he saw the gentle rise and fall of her sleeping form underneath the teal bed spread. She's still asleep. Good he didn't need her bull shit on top of everything else. He was depressed enough.

Absent-mindedly he chewed on a finger nail from his right hand as he stared out the large picture window at the heavy raindrops falling from the low overcast. The larger clearer drops that were visible to the naked eye sped past on their journey to the red brick walkway he knew was far below his field of vision. The light from the room caused speeding to their inevitable doom. Much like his own life at this moment.

His glossy, black leather uniform shoes shone in the early evening light. It would soon be time wake Rose. His four to six respite was about to expire.

The city, once vibrant with life, looked dead to him. The colorful array of lights that met his gaze offered him

No joy.

Melancholy musings were interrupted by a burst of sound being emitted by the beige phone sitting on the brown laminate end table next to the queen bed. An identical end table stood on the opposite side to complete the set.

He couldn't will himself to move before Rose, rising on one elbow, her pink and blue flannel night shirt rumpled from her involuntary night tremors picked up the receiver from its cradle.

"Yes," she said into mouth piece, her voice edged with sleep.

Jack heard the echo of someone speaking then Rose sat suddenly bolt up right her eyes wide in wonder. For a second he thought she'd had a heart attack from the way her face drained of blood. The conversation finished with her acknowledging the caller and replacing the receiver with a sharp click.

She threw back the covers with her usual flourish and, after swinging her short legs so they were hanging above the charcoal gray carpet, and shifting her weight forward, she stepped barefoot onto the carpet next to the bed.

"I've got to get dressed. We have an appointment downstairs." Her voice was hard, and her gray eyes were filled with determination, her jaw clenched.

He stared at her unable to fathom what she was talking about. She walked toward the bathroom where she kept her makeup. "Why?" was all he managed to say behind her.

"There's been a murder."

Cape Disappointment

Her voice echoed from inside the pale peach three piece bathroom common to most hotels. The words hung in the air as he broke into a cold sweat beneath his navy gold shit which he was now glad he'd put in place of the light red one. A sense of dread gripped him to replace his melancholy mood of moments before.

"What has this got to do with us? I'm on vacation, for God's sake."

"The cop said the dead person is an old girl friend of yours. Kelly somebody or other."

10

Ben sat with his black raincoat tossed across his left arm with his fingers locked together in his lap in the tight, ornately carved, low backed chair. It was the type of furniture he hated. It had wooden arms that cut into his side.

He distracted himself by studying the people going to and fro in the lobby. Being a trained detective he enjoyed studying the various people as they rushed by him.

His ability to make a living is based solely on his skill at observation, consequently. When the opportunity to practice presented itself he'd sit and watch people to see how they interacted with each other. It helped him keep his edge as detective .

The writer's convention currently going on at this hotel was a prime candidate worthy of his study. These people were unique.

Presently he had his eye on a middle aged bleached blonde wearing a green fake satin dress, an imitation fix fur slung around her neck, and a white floppy hat with an ornate pink feather sticking from the top.

Tethered at the double leash in her right hand were two miniature schnauzers.

Cape Disappointment

The leash had been shortened to restrict the dogs movements and prevent them to stray too far.

From what he could tell from the direction she was headed she was about to run headlong into the hotel manager. The manager's reaction at seeing her dogs should be educational and fun at the same time.

What would've been a very entertaining moment ended when Rose Thomas trailed by her husband, Jack, appeared from one of the elevator as it disgorged passengers into the carpeted lobby area. Being the only black man in the place made their recognition of him pretty much a given. Similarly their expressions told him they knew who he was.

Ben's round belly jiggled beneath his white shirt as he pushed himself forward with both hands to escape the grip of the prison he found himself in.

Many times he'd thought about offing the person who'd made these chairs. They were so lacking when it came to comfort or practicality. Of course, they also discouraged people from hanging around hotel lobby's creating problems for him and his brothers and sisters on the force.

He held his striped red tie down over his tailored navy wool suit as he stood to greet the Thomas'.

Jack Thomas held out his hand and his narrow face broke into a wide grin.

From his research at the station before coming to speak with them Ben knew Jack was a small town cop in Ontario, which made the news he had to deliver that much more complicated than he would've wished.

Rose Thomas however was another matter. Her thin lips and corpulent frame made her appear doughy. The heavy black frame of her glasses hanging off her long nose reminded him of his third grade teacher back in grammar school.

Apparently she was some kind of poet. Ben knew nothing about poetry or poets, but for some reason she looked every bit the part as far as he was concerned.

Ben held out his hand and after gripping Jack's found it was firm and solid. He did notice his hand was moist indicating he either sweat a lot naturally or was nervous.

Rose appeared somewhat indignant about having to meet with him.

"Perhaps we should go somewhere private?" said Ben casting his gaze on Jack.

Rose glared at him her eyes filled with rage. "I knew it. We could have stayed in our room and done this." Her tone said cold bitch and reminded Ben of his ex.

"Actually, a forensic team is going over your room as we speak," Ben said trying to sound apologetic.

"You think we had something to do with the woman's death. It was an accident wasn't it?" Rose folded her arms across the rise of her large breasts. Her white sport sock clad feet, sealed in green and gray plaid bedroom slippers, shuffled back and forth as she spoke.

"I didn't mean..."

"What are you saying?" Rose interrupted him. Her posture was straight and her green unyielding eyes focused on his black ones

Ben frowned, placed his right hand in his trouser pocket, then changed gears. He decided to modify his tone and information sharing to elicit an emotional response, one he could weight and measure. The detection game was truth and dare. He'd used this technique many times to find the liar among the range of suspects.

In this case there were so many loop holes, and suspects, he knew it wasn't going to an easy case. This bitch was making it even harder with this attitude. If she wanted to dance then so be it, start the music.

He lowered his voice as he stared his face a mask of patience. "Mrs. Thomas, I am trying to eliminate suspects. True you didn't know the victim but you're husband did. At one time," he added.

R.G. Crossley

Her eyes went wide and she turned to face Jack who visibly shrunk. The smile disappeared from the small town cop's features since the conversation had turned. Up to this point Ben thought he seemed to be enjoying his wife's antics now that her focus was off him.

Ben, watching the woman's face turn an unimaginable mixture of shades of purple and red before she would unload on the guy, decided he better in to save the poor guy's ass.

"At this point I also don't believe he actually did it. My suspects usually have far greater reasons for murder than unrequited love. Seeing as you're a writer this is a terrible clichéd idea don't you think?"

This appeared to stop her in her tracks. He'd hit her where she lived. Her ego wasn't about to be bruised. Of course she knew that old standby, and since her husband was a cop, the idea was unthinkable and even more of a silly notion.

Her pallor returned to its previous pale complexion as she thought about what Ben had just said. For a few seconds she stood still her face frozen with the expression of someone deep in thought, her eyes flitted back and forth (the wheels of her mind obviously turning.)

Finally she, her shoulders slumped ever so slightly, straightened her suit jacket, and after making an attempt to rip from her head one of the short mousy brown curls of hair hovering over her left ear, as if in some kind of bizarre torture ritual, she made up her mind. He thought for a second she might actually yank the curl, roots and all, out of her scalp like a cork screw if she pulled hard enough, but she managed to let her do live to fight another day.

"Is there anything else?" Her tone suggested defeat. It was clear the lady didn't enjoy losing.

"Yes, I need to talk to your husband alone."

Rose glanced at Jack then red faced, and still twisting furiously at the curl of loose hair, turned. She hurried away like Canada geese being chased by toddlers in some public park. With a flash of the green slacks, he concluded no doubt part of an ensemble, she disappeared into the restaurant.

Jack watched her go his face the symbol of calm. When she was out of sight he broke down and laughed. Tears streamed down his cheeks, and the no doubt hard won paunch of his stomach shook.

Ben smiled to himself. He and Jack had more in common than being policemen.

"Boy, you really showed her." Jack managed to choke the words out between guffaws.

Ben withdrew his right hand from his trousers. He reached inside his suit jacket pocket to pull out his notebook. He flipped it to a blank page and began to write something with a black and white ball point pen. As Jack watched Ben's actions his laughter subsided until he realized what this meant.

"You're going to arrest me aren't you?"

"Yup." Ben reached behind his navy suit jacket and pulled his metal handcuffs from the hidden pouch he kept there. Some guys liked to wear the pouch on their side he like to keep it hidden. In his opinion it was less intimidating and made soliciting much needed investigative information easier. Now he needed them.

The act of pulling back the jacket to revealed his gold detective's badge on the right front of his belt near to the left of the trouser pocket made the color drain from Ben's face.

Being polished to a high sheen the cuffs glowed in the late afternoon light streaming thought the double skylights forty feet overhead. Even in winter the sky would be sometimes bright from stray rays of sunlight that managed to escape through the overcast. Even on one those dull, gray Vancouver winter days.

Ben clipped the first ring around Jack's wrist accompanied immediately by the ratcheting sound as they were locked into place.

After getting Jack to turn his back to him, Ben slipped the other one around his remaining wrist. He then pulled the man's arms together in the approved position, slipped the end into the locking mechanism and completed the job.

He knew from his year at the Ontario police college in Brampton that he had little hope of proving his innocence. The evidence was purely circumstantial, but he realized he'd left a trail of phone calls, answering machine recordings and love notes a mile wide. He knew he didn't kill her, he loved her.

By this time a crowd of curiosity seekers had gathered to watch. As Ben read him his rights his deep voice echoing on his unfocussed hearing Jack's bladder let loose with a flood of piss that soaked through his clothes to run down the inside of his pant legs.

Ben finished reading the warning and caution from his brown leather notebook then replaced it inside his jacket pocket.

As he led Jack away Ben heard a voice say, "Hey look, the stupid bastard peed himself." Followed immediately by gales of laughter.

11

Ben, having changed into tattered blue jeans and a white tee shirt, leaned back only to sink into the over stuffed couch facing the large picture over looking the harbor.

He shared his one room apartment with his cat, Jessie, a little white and orange tabby he'd found wandering the streets near his building some months before.

Jessie sat at his feet quietly licking her paws.

He lifted the cold beer can to his lips. After taking a swallow to cool his aching throat he set the can on the light colored pine coffee table. The unused cardboard coasters with little gold anchors imprinted on them sat unused stacked in the center of the table.

His empty gaze stared at the white, red, and yellow harbor lights that dotted the shoreline. Kelly was dead and there was nothing he could have done to prevent it.

Jack would be released tomorrow after the captain found the file folder missing. No evidence. No case. That was the rule.

He let the whisper of a sigh escape between his lips then reached for the beer can to take another blast. Oblivion had to be better than this.

For a second he wondered who had killed her.

He didn't care but the detective in him, that special something that made him the love to solve mysteries something that he was good at, begged to be let free. He suppressed the thought immediately.

She was a whore and deserved to be dead.

He'd been waiting since the seventies to find the right opportunity. When Mrs. Thomas had called him from Toronto to tell him her and her husband would be in Vancouver he couldn't pass up the chance.

His career would be over, but what the hell. Maybe he'd become a fry cook at some greasy spoon, or maybe a pool hustler after all. He was pretty good with the stick.

The restaurant manager. Now there was a sleazy piece of work.

A good frame up candidate. But the slime balls criminal record went back twenty years, and mostly for petty crimes, not anything with violence. Who would believe he'd graduated to murder after all this time.

Hard to believe the guy wanted to be a writer, which explained his meeting with the agent at the same hotel as Jack was staying.

And the dishwasher. He had served time for drug dealing. Small time stuff mostly.

Naw, the small town cop, the captain really loved that one. Ben had made his captain an easy believer based on that fact. It was the case closer if there ever was one.

A thought suddenly occurred to him. Maybe the fat broad killed Kelly. He started to chuckle at his own joke.

Jessie stopped licking herself to stare up at him probably wondering what was so funny.

He shook his head. Naw, the poet was too esoteric to kill anyone.

Cape Disappointment

Rose closed her notebook after she drew a straight blue line through the last item on her list.

She smiled to herself. Done. Ten years of planning were complete.

Jack would never suspect. And besides he was too stupid to realize how she'd done it.

Ben would make sure he made it home and all once more would be right with the world. More importantly the rules were meant to be obeyed.

If only Jack hadn't made that call like she knew he would, (he was so predictable). Maybe then none of this would've happened, and the little scheming bitch would still be alive.

The note she'd left for Jack to find had been a clue of inspired genius. Damn that Ben Harris is a clever man.

Kelly herself was no dummy, but not as clever as her. Rose kept to her rules. Consequently Cape Disappointment had claimed another victim.

The heavily loaded 747 shook as it lumbered down the runway then into the winter sky to take her home and away from her disappointment.

No man would break the rules on her watch ever again.

The Watcher of Wayburn Street

I TOOK A SIP OF THE HOT coffee and winced when it burned against my tongue. I should have waited for it cool down.

I look out the large picture window to see a man wearing a soiled powder blue track suit, his hair the color of steel wool, pushing a rusted grocery cart brimming with dumpster treasurers in the crosswalk on Wayburn Street.

I see the usual drug dealers on the other side of the street peddling their wares outside the abandoned fruit and vegetable store. In the dirty window of delicatessen next door one end of the GOING OUT OF BUSINESS sign hangs limp as it has for over a year.

The Watcher of Wayburn Street

I watched as cars, trucks and buses from the suburbs whizzed past another grizzled street veteran sitting hunchback-like on the cracked sidewalk, until the traffic light over the intersection warns them to stop. It changes to yellow, followed a few seconds later, to red.

Airbrakes sigh and brakes squeal as the hurried occupants of the assorted vehicles applied brakes and traffic comes to a stop. I watched the light over Wayburn change to green then northbound trucks, cars and buses leap forward like an unleashed dog to stream away.

This flotsam of traffic will continue all day, just as it has every day for the past eighteen years.

"Hi, Mr. Kenniphaas."

I look up to find Autumn Siu standing over me smiling warmly. She's a college student who works as a part time barista. Her dark eyes gaze at me and she seems pleased as usual to see me. Autumn, no more than twenty years old, her shoulder length rich black hair tied behind her oval shaped head into a pony tail, is busy clearing tables.

When she started working at Coffee Planet she made a point to learn the names of the regulars. Unlike me, Autumn is destined to go far in life with that attitude.

"Good morning, Autumn." I smiled as I rested my gnarled hands on the end of the brass handle of my cane.

"See anything interesting today?"

I chuckled drily. "No, not today." I lowered my voice. "But you should have seen yesterday." I wiggled my bushy white eyebrows comically.

Her laugh was like a wind chime. "Oh, Mr. Kenniphaas, you are so silly." With another laugh she walked away pushing a cart with a plastic dish tub on top. I watched her busily plucking empty coffee cups, plates covered in muffin crumbs and flakes of pastry, and crumpled napkins, off the round oak tables scattered through out the dimly lit coffee shop. The dishes rattled as the cart rolled over the brown-and-gray textured floor tiles.

"Cinnamon latté," Jessie Walker, a willowy blonde, called from behind the chest-high drink station where the specialty coffees were prepared.

Tamber Lickiss, heavy-set with shoulder-length hair the color of sun bleached seashells, dressed in tattered blue jeans and new white Nikes, waddled to the counter and snatched the paper cup with the Saturn-shaped logo on the side. The strong odor of cinnamon filled my senses from my seat on the other side of the shop.

The Watcher of Wayburn Street

I knew Tamber well. She had been my cleaning lady until three months ago when I caught her stealing. Tamber was a nice young woman, but lazy, and I suspect has a problem with alcohol, or perhaps something worse.

At first she denied lifting the money from my wallet until I showed her the bank slip with the sixty dollars I'd withdrawn that morning. When confronted with the fact my wallet now contained only forty dollars she admitted her guilt.

I felt pity for her and told her I wouldn't involve the police and said she was to keep the twenty dollars as severance pay. Involving the police would involve the outside world. I preferred to handle such matters privately.

She seemed grateful, but two weeks later she bad mouthed me in front of her friends when we encountered each other at Planet Coffee. Her language revealed a solid understanding of street life, but her grammar was atrocious and her reference to me as a lover of swine was puzzling. She even threatened me with bodily harm, as if I had done something awful to her.

At first I was annoyed she would embarrass me at my coffee shop, but I let it go. No confrontation is worth it. I forgave her.

I watched Tamber take the cup, and heard her too-many-cigarettes-damaged voice complain about the lack of foam on the coffee.

After Jessie explained the amount of foam was standard, Tamber grunted, then begrudgingly walked away and headed for the door leading to the small parking lot next to the shop. Her sea-green eyes narrowed to slits as she scuffed past me. The tinny bell above the door rang brightly when it closed behind her.

I was surprised when my shoulders relaxed now that she was gone. Was I really afraid of her? I shrugged and went back to watching the bank located diagonally across the street from the coffee shop.

Autumn had indeed missed the excitement yesterday. I didn't tell her about it because she might worry and what good would that do?

***

Yesterday, fifteen minutes after I'd sat at my usual table, a large black car with spinning chrome wheels and tinted windows pulled up in front of the bank. Three men exited the still running car with balaclavas covering their faces. They were dressed head-to-toe in black and they each carried a pistol in one hand, and a pillow case in the other.

I recall thinking it odd one of the pillowcases had a flowery pattern.

The men entered the bank.

The robbers were back in a few minutes, the pillow cases bulging, and quickly disappeared into the car.

Planet Coffee's windows shimmered when the car's powerful engine roared and then it sped away with a squeal of tires, leaving behind a cloud of blue smoke.

Within seconds I heard the wail of sirens headed this way. A plethora of police cars soon arrived to close the intersection.

It was then I spotted Tamber appear from the alley behind the bank. She was talking on her cell phone and a wide grin split her freckled features.

Even though I couldn't hear what she was saying there was something in the way she talked that made me curious. She seemed excited and her eyes scanned the growing throng of the curious, and the cops in their navy blue uniforms, as if she were enjoying the mayhem caused by the bank robbery.

Lastly, an unmarked car, with a red flashing light on its slate-gray roof, stopped in front of the bank entrance. A tall white-haired man exited the passenger side, while a younger blonde woman, her eyes hidden by dark sunglasses, exited the driver's side. They both wore navy blue suits, white shirts, neither wore a tie.

I could see the bulge in their jackets made by a gun on their hips. When a breeze briefly caused their jackets to billow open I saw a flash of sunlight off the gold badges on their belts.

The two detectives went to the sidewalk and began a conversation with a statesman-like uniformed policeman holding a portable radio in his left hand. There were gold bars on the collar of his uniform shirt. They spoke for several minutes then the woman swivelled her head to face the coffee shop. She turned back to the two men then nodded and headed for the crosswalk.

She was coming here to interview witnesses. I considering leaving before she arrived, then immediately dismissed the idea when she broke into a trot, and I saw two uniformed behemoths had moved to guard the coffee shop's only door.

My hands trembled. No one was leaving, including me.

***

Her name was Emily Harris, Detective, Third Grade. Her tone was surprisingly gentle as I listened and watched her question each person in the shop until she got to me.

My table faced the bank. I was the best witness. I was the one she really wanted to interview.

I noticed her eyes flit to me several times during her interviews with the others. I felt a single bead of perspiration run down the side of my face. I was afraid to wipe it away.

But I realized she'd made a mistake. She questioned everyone together rather than separately. I'd watched enough cop shows to know the procedures. Divide and conquer was standard police practice.

What I failed to consider was no one here was involved in the robbery. We weren't suspects we were witnesses.

Once it was my turn I discovered Emily's intelligent hazel eyes were kind and her voice was dry and she was a good listener.

I told her everything I'd seen describing the car, the robbers, and pillow cases. Her brow wrinkled slightly as I told her about the pattern on one of the pillow cases.

"That's important isn't it?" I'd provided what I considered a salient fact.

Emily shrugged her right shoulder. "Hard to say. Could be."

To say I was disappointed falls far short of how I deflated I felt at that moment.

Sensing my disappointment she changed subjects. "What do you do?"

144

Emily (she encouraged me to call her Emily) fingered the page of the notebook open on the table in front of as her curious eyes studied me. A black pen lay on the table next to the book. After she'd recorded my name, address, and other tombstone data, she'd put the pen down and crossed her legs.

"I used to teach high school English."

Her eyes widened. "Really? How long ago?"

"Eighteen years."

The corners of her mouth curled. "That long, huh?" I nodded. She swivelled her head to look at her fellow cops setting up a band of banana-yellow tape to bar the unwanted from entering the bank then she looked back at me. "What do you do now?"

Without pausing to consider my words I responded. "I watch."

Her eyebrows arched. "Really?" She nodded toward the parking lot to my left on the other side of the window. "Out there?"

"Yes. Huh...I mean the world..." I shrugged and forced my mouth to form a grin. "I mean not the whole world just Wayburn Street."

She smiled. "You're the watcher of Wayburn Street, huh?"

"I guess that'd be the best way to describe me."

Emily uncrossed her legs and shifted forward on the wooden chair. "So tell me, who did you see doing something unusual at the time of the robbery?"

I wondered how she knew. "Huh, there's this woman..."

"A woman?" Her brow creased.

"Huh, yes. Tamber Lickiss. She was talking on her cell phone right after the robbery."

Emily sat back in her chair and frowned. "And why is this important?"

I realized I was going to sound silly. "Tamber was talking funny." She raised one eyebrow. "I mean, she was laughing and joking."

"People laugh and joke on cell phones every day. What makes this different?"

I hesitated. <u>Do I tell her</u>? "Tamber stole money from me," I explained at last.

After a few more questions about Tamber, and where she lived, Emily thanked me and I headed home secure in the knowledge I'd done the right thing.

Today, though, Tamber made me nervous. Why should I be nervous? It's not like I knew for sure she had anything to do with the bank robbery.

I was lost in my own world when a voice jolted me back to reality. "Mr. Kenniphaas?"

I looked up and it was Autumn again, this time with a steaming mug of coffee in one hand. "I noticed your coffee was cold and thought you'd want a fresh one."

I smiled and glanced down at the half empty mug in front of me. Just as she said it was cold and thoroughly unappealing. I looked back at her. "Thank you, Autumn. You are a dear."

She smiled, set the mug on the table, and picked up the old one. I reached for my wallet.

Autumn held up one hand. "No charge, Mr. Kenniphaas."

I smiled at her. "Thank you again."

"No worries," Autumn said with a giggle as she spun round and disappeared in the direction of the washrooms. I glanced at my watch. 11:30. Washroom inspection time. I smiled to myself. The girl was certainly conscientious. Like I said she's destined to go far.

I started when the door to the parking lot burst inward to bang hard against the condiment stand.

A knot formed in my stomach as I watched Tamber Lickiss enter, her features twisted in a sneer, her eyes filled with an unearthly rage. She was breathing hard and the fingers of her right hand gripped a large hunting knife.

She went directly to the counter. "Give me the money," she growled at Jerry Smalls who stood behind the counter. She held up the knife to emphasize her demand.

There were two other people besides me in the coffee shop. Helen Madras, in her blue dental assistant's uniform, and a young man I didn't recognize with a goatee and long auburn hair that drooped across his shoulders. They were both frozen apparently unable to move.

Jerry's features were ashen and his hands trembled as he fumbled with the cash register's buttons trying to open it.

"Hurry it up or your dead," threatened Tamber wielding the knife at poor frightened Jerry.

Finally, Jerry managed to open the drawer. "Step back," commanded Tamber. He did. She rose on the toes of her sneakers and peered into the tray. She snorted her disgust. "That's it? It isn't enough to buy cat food."

Spinning around her hard eyes travelled over Helen and the long haired boy. "Give 'em your wallets," she grunted.

This made Helen and the boy finally move. They had their wallets on the table within seconds.

Tamber snatched Helen's wallet from the table.

Still holding the knife in one hand she opened Helen's wallet and a twisted smiled crossed her features. "Now this is more like it." She pulled out five one hundred dollar bills stuffed them in the pocket of her jeans then let Helen's wallet drop to the floor with a <u>smack</u>.

"That's rent money," Helen whispered.

Tamber glared at her. "Keep talkin', lady, and you won't have to worry about rent.

Helen averted her eyes as her shoulders slumped and she began to sob.

"Hey! What's going on?" Autumn?

Tamber swung round the knife held waist high. The tip of the blade made contact with Autumn's shirt and tore a rip across her belly.

I don't remember much of what happened next. I do have a foggy memory of a sickening odor of cigarettes and stale beer.

They tell me I lost it. Apparently I shouted Autumn's name as I struck Tamber's hand with the handle of my cane and managed to knock the knife free. It fell to the floor with a clatter. I'm told I broke her wrist.

I felt bad about hurting her.

The kid with the goatee and the long hair turned out to be an uncover cop who arrested Tamber.

149

The next thing I recall was sitting at my usual table at Coffee Planet across from a smiling Detective Emily Harris.

"You okay?"

"Yes, I think so, Emily." I blinked away the fog clouding my brain. "What happened?"

"We got the bank robbers." I nodded. "And as you suspected Tamber was involved. She was the lookout."

"Oh. Really?" I narrowed my eyes. "What's going to happen to her?"

Emily's pencil thin eyebrows rose. "She's been charged as an accomplice in the bank robbery, and with the attempted armed robbery of this coffee shop." She shrugged. "I expect she's going to be going away for a long time."

I looked around and realized Helen, Jerry, Autumn, and the long haired kid were gone. "Where is everyone?"

"They finished their statements so I had a constable drive them home."

My heart rate increased. "Then Autumn's ok?"

Emily's mouth curled at the corners as before. "She's fine, but she'll have to buy another shirt." I nodded as the tension in my shoulders eased and my heart rate returned to normal. She added, "You're quite the hero ya know?"

I shook my head. "No. Not me. I watch. I don't get involved."

Emily reached out to pat the back of my hand and chuckled. "No, sorry, Mr. Kenniphaas, you're now officially the hero of Wayburn Street."

I knew she was right. The world had changed.

"You want me to add a charge of robbery for the money she stole from you?"

I looked into her hazel eyes and saw she was serious. "No, of course not."

She frowned. "Why not?"

"I already forgave her for that."

One eyebrow shot up on Emily's forehead. "And what about today? Are you going to forgive her for today?"

"Yes, of course. And I'll visit her in jail. She needs help."

Emily shook her head and stood. "Okay, Mr. Kenniphaas. I'll give you a ride home."

We walked outside into the small parking lot to be greeted by a light rain. For the first time I noticed my clothes reeked of stale coffee.

I spend far too much time in this coffee shop hiding from life.

The buzz of traffic on Wayburn Street filled my senses as Emily opened the passenger side door of the unmarked police car.

"Tamber said she was going to hurt you," said Emily as I sank into the passenger seat of the large sedan.

Before I could respond she closed the car door and walked around the hood of the car. I adjusted my weight as I sank into the plush cloth seat, sighed, and shut my eyes.

I smiled to myself. Emily's right, the watcher of Wayburn Street is officially retired. And I wasn't afraid of Tamber or anyone else.

I had become the hero of my own story. I wasn't going to stand by and just watch anymore. It was time to change the world.

A Day Without Sunshine

IT SEEMS EVERY TIME I smell blood it's a good day.

The iron smell of the dark ruby liquid means I'm going to pay my rent, and maybe even eat. For sure my bartender is happy because I'll settle my tab. As it turned out however this blood was the start of the worst day of my life.

Today I found her body in a pool of blood in the hallway outside my dingy office door. Since I hadn't had my morning coffee her death gave me a sour stomach. And I hate a sour stomach.

Hell of a day to quit smoking. Before I quit the weed the first cigarette of the day masked the smells of the putrid mornings in my world. But not today.

A Day Without Sunshine

In my line of work a dead mystery woman is just another day at the office except this was a rich broad. You know the type, a gal from the right side of the tracks who lives to visit the wrong side for the excitement.

I was born, live, and have always worked, on the wrong side of the tracks so I fully expect to die on the wrong side. The hourglass-shaped, copper-haired woman that lay dead on my doorstep had beat me to the other side.

Problem was a woman dressed in an Anna Sui Organza cocktail dress in this part of town was a like a neon sign that reads FREE SAMPLES. (Good thing every gray organza cocktail dress, with a black tulle layer and sequin embroidery, has a label under the neck line just like any off-the-shelf-Wal-Mart knockoff)

In the circumstances it wasn't a surprise she was murdered--and had her no doubt matching handbag stolen--but why did she have to die on my doorstep, with my business card gripped in the pale lifeless fingers of her left hand? She'd found her excitement but now I was somehow involved, and I didn't know why. I really hate it when I don't know why. Guess that's why I became a PI.

After I'd made the call to my homicide contact, Inspector Lyle Crowder, to notify him of the untimely death,

I stood over the corpse in order to study her closely.

Her natural red hair looked freshly permed, and her cinnamon tinged perfume masked the usual door of urine and decay prevalent in the three story brick walk up I call my home away from home. Though my definition of home is fluid.

The twenty-year old overstuffed couch in my two-room rented office had depressions that matched my lean frame. I'd only been sleeping on it for the past nine months and already it fit like a glove.

High cheekbones and lightly applied makeup made her beautiful in my eyes. Her legs—long and shapely—were accentuated by slightly muscular calves. She obviously worked out, but not so much as to become the female version of Governor Arnie. I think the exercise gurus call it body sculpting. Her appearance suggested she had a personal trainer. I have a personal trainer too. My bartender, Mickey Risk, ensures I bend my elbow on a daily basis.

Crowder appeared in the hallway accompanied by his partner Wally Esper. I don't care much for Wally. His appearance reminds of a weasel, with a personality and attitude to match. It was the same in every town I drifted into. The good homicide dicks always seemed to have weasels for partners.

A Day Without Sunshine

And I loath every one of 'em.

Wally's beady eyes narrowed as he realized it was me who'd called them out so early in the a.m. I nodded to the two cops as they came up to stand beside me over the redhead's lifeless corpse.

Crowder looked painfully thin in his baggy standard cop issue cheap dark blue suit, white shirt, and narrow black tie. His bald head was covered by an ink-black fedora. I'm glad hats for men have made a comeback. Sam Spade would be proud.

Not that I was much better in my only five-year-old pinstriped navy suit that had seen better days. My thin dark tie was loose at the unbuttoned collar of my one clean white shirt. I may only have one suit and tie but at least I own four white shirts. Like Lyle I usually wear my fedora when I go out. Sure, it's chocolate brown, and clashes with my suit, but then I'm no slave to fashion.

I smelled the cigarette Lyle had just finished—I felt a twinge of envy. The tobacco smoke mingled with Wally's drug store aftershave. The weasel didn't have to get all dolled up just for little 'ol me.

"Hey, Stiletto," said Lyle, in his patented bored style meant to disarm the suspect.

Naturally I expected to be considered a suspect. After all an ex-cop who'd made some mistakes on the job was the perfect patsy. But I also knew Lyle would find any excuse to eliminate me from his mental checklist. He knew I wasn't the cold-blooded killer type.

Sure I'm a screw up, but I'd certainly never murder anyone. He also knew I had a nose for the less than obvious clues that have so often resulted in the bad guy riding old sparky into the next world. And Lyle lived for convictions. Besides I'd rather love 'em than kill 'em, especially with a looker like the dead redhead sprawled across the scarred wooden floor boards.

All I needed to do was help him to eliminate me from his usual suspects list. "Hey, Crowder...Esper," I added, nodding to Wally who grimaced as he stuffed his hands in the pockets of his cheap brown suit pants and rocked back slightly on his heels.

"Had your coffee yet?" asked Crowder as his analytical blue eyes scanned the redhead's body.

"Nope."

Crowder nodded. "Too bad. Me neither."

"Don't you ever shave?" Lyle quipped eyeing my four days growth of beard.

"Once a week, whether I need to or not," I said.

Lyle chuckled then sank to his haunches and peered hard at my business card held in her fingers. He grunted. "Looks like a plant to me."

Esper snorted and opened his mouth to speak.

Lyle shot him a look. Wally's wide mouth snapped shut and he appeared properly cowed. I wanted to smile at the weasels discomfort but held back.

"Throat cut. Too bad." He shook his head. "Rich dame," added Lyle before rising to stand and stuffed his hands in his pants pockets. He'd drawn the same conclusion I had from her makeup and clothes. He glanced at me. "Any handbag?" I shook my head.

"Uh, uh…" A frown creased his forehead. "Know her?"

"Never saw her before I stepped outta my office door this morning—"

"Did you hear sumthing…kinda early…" He was right. It was only five in the a.m.

I shook my head. "Nope. I was going to the corner, to that twenty-four/seven coffee shop…"

"Huh, huh…" He tipped his hat back slightly on his head with his right index finger. "Wally, when are the crime scene boys gonna be here?" he said, not taking eyes off the victim.

Wally's eyes shifted to me then back to his boss. "Uhhh…I don't know…"

"Find out," said Crowder. "Go down to the street and show 'em the way up here."

"But it's raining," whined the weasel.

Crowder cast his cool gaze over Wally who

nodded sheepishly then, without another word, walked away down the hall to the stairs. His heavy footsteps echoed on the squeaky wooden planks until they faded as he disappeared down the stairs. My shabby office was on the third floor.

Now that we were alone, Lyle's shoulders relaxed and he looked at me, his blue eyes steady with an edge of the curious common to most detectives.

"You piss someone off lately?" he said, his tone suggested more of a statement than a question.

I shrugged my shoulders. Truth was I was always pissing someone off. The job description of a private dick includes an innate ability to piss people off at least once a week without getting killed. Problem was this was a rich broad, and if someone with bucks to burn wanted me dead they could have hired a pro and taken me out five minutes after the check cleared.

"The usual suspects; drug dealers, cheating husbands, pimps, and other assorted bottom feeders not worth mentioning." I shook my head. "No one in her league, that's for sure."

Lyle frowned. He stepped toward me and placed one hand on my left shoulder. "Listen, Jazz, I know you only been in town for nine months, and we don't know each other too well, but if there's something you're not telling me..." He let his words hang for several seconds his sympathetic eyes locked on mine then he added, "I'd hate to see you murdered too."

A lightning bolt of realization struck me. "Who's dead?" I asked slowly.

Lyle dropped his hands to his side and he leaned against the hallway wall compressing the peeling yellowed wallpaper with his bulky frame. His eyes dropped to the floor his chin on his chest.

"We found Bobbi Diamond last night," he said, his baritone voice just above a whisper. Lyle slashed his index finger across his throat to demonstrate Bobbi had been killed in the same fashion as our mystery woman.

I knew Diamond. She was a rival PI who had an office over on Carpenter Park Drive. She had four PI's under contract working for her. Too often I'd thought about applying to be one of them, but my gut was telling me I was gone, gone, gone---and soon. I had never made it a year in one place before I got the itch to get outta Dodge.

Diamond's crew took on cases so far out of my league they might as well be on another planet. Her cases usually involved the elite movers and shakers of the city. The papers were chock full of divorce hurricanes between the rich and powerful, and Diamond's PI agency was usually at the eye of those storms.

"Cap's on my ass to snag Diamond's killer."

I smirked. "Yeah, I know."

Everyone on the street knew Diamond had done the chief of the PD a favour. Her operatives had delivered naughty pics of the chief's wife and a city councilman doing the nasty. Rumor was the chief pulled some strings, and the judge who granted him the divorce had sealed the court records never to be make their way to public eyes.

Unfortunately, some of the more revealing pictures—with black lines over the naughty bits—were splashed across the morning paper two days ago. The editor claimed the pictures were delivered by a courier, and he claimed the return address was an empty lot.

"Let's get that coffee," I suggested. Crowder heaved a heavy sigh and nodded. I liked this guy. I wanted to help him.

***

We were seated at one of three dark stained wooden tables, dotted with mug rings, each with a steaming cup of mountain grown goodness in front of us. Another thing Lyle and I had in common we both drank our coffee black.

I closed my eyes and took a sip of the hot brew. The aromatic earthiness of the fresh roasted beans cleared my senses of death. I made a yummy sound and smirked.

I opened my eyes to see Lyle's attention was on the street.

I almost spewed the coffee across the table. He was looking in the direction of a white limousine that had stopped in front of my building. Since when did limousines stop in front of my building? This didn't look good even to me, and I knew I'd done nothing wrong.

The driver, a giant of a black man dressed in an ink-black chauffeur's uniform complete with the cap and white shirt and matching tie, was right out Driving Miss Daisy. Except this guy was no Morgan Freeman. He had a bull neck and a forehead that hung low over coal hard eyes. From his left ear, at the end of a gold chain, dangled a brilliant diamond that would have made Liz Taylor envious. His suit jacket bulged from the rippling muscles barely contain by the expensive fabric. It seemed body guard/chauffeur work paid better than licensed private detective.

Maybe I should...naw, I enjoy my freedom too much.

"Looks like you got visitors," said Lyle, his eyes focused on the long white car that seemed to cover the half block.

My building sat in the middle of the block. Lyle turned his cool gaze on me, his blue eyes were like twin lamps the old-time movie cops used to interrogate suspects.

I looked away from Lyle's quizzical eyes in time to see the driver walk up to weasel-boy Wally. Watching the big man tower over the cheap detective I felt a pleasant sensation. Wally looked scared of the big guy. Good for you, body guard guy.

The passenger was obviously going to wait curb side in the comfort of the luxury box on wheels while the driver fetched me. How did I know it was me they were looking for you ask? Given a choice of occupants of a dilapidated building that included an importer of dime store trinkets, assorted crack dealers, and one slightly rumpled private dick, who else could it be? Especially with one of their own kind found dead outside my office.

When I looked back Lyle had dropped his gaze to the mug of steaming coffee in front of him. "I think you better go talk to them. I suspect they won't be too eager to talk to me."

"Yeah," I agreed. I got up from the table and started for the door.

"Oh, and Jazz…" I stopped and swivelled my eyes to his, which had fixed themselves on me.

A Day Without Sunshine

"Anything you find out...?" He didn't need to finish the sentence. He had cut me some slack to get to the bottom of this mess. After all, the dead girl had my business card in her fingers when she was found and now someone who probably loved her had shown up.

Sure, Lyle could have run us all in and held everyone until someone talked, but he knew I'd get to the bottom of the case faster if I was out. After all I had done it before. And he knew I'd share anything I found out with him. He knows I'm reliable. Lyle is a good cop with unparalleled instincts for people. I nodded and exited the coffee shop.

I walked toward the limo with its dark shaded windows and felt unseen eyes study me. The bodyguard who had been cowing Wally turned to look at me. His dark emotionless eyes narrowed slightly. He ignored Wally and moved to stand on guard beside the long car his hands folded in front of him.

As I approached the passenger door the window slid down with a soft burr. The car's seats were covered in wine-red leather. Once beside the car I discovered the passenger was a woman dressed in black , a pale complexion, and brilliant blue eyes. She studied me up and down as I stared open mouthed at her. High cheekbones and long chestnut brown hair famed a face that only God could have made.

The neckline of her dress ended at the base of her long tapered neck, and the slight swell of her bosom was covered a strand of ivory white pearls each flawless and exactly the same size and shape. Her matching pearl earrings adorned her perfectly shaped ear lobes. She would be the ideal model for the Venus Di Milo.

"Mr. Stiletto?" she said softly. Her voice reminded me of the sound of a summer breeze, with an edge of huskiness that would wake a dead man. I felt a stir in my loins but forced the dirty thoughts away by clearing my throat.

"Ahem...yes, I'm Stiletto...Jazz Stiletto..."

"I understand my sister was found dead outside your office this morning."

***

After the ride in Ms. Penny-Anne Robespierre's — of the Rhode Island Robespierre's — stretch limousine I felt somewhat revived. The form fitted seat that encased my weary body like a cocoon, combined with the strong coffee, had managed to revive me for what was sure to be a fun filled day. That is if your definition of fun includes murder, secrets, and lies.

Rich people and their games. These people have too much time on their hands.

A Day Without Sunshine

The car finally stopped outside a mansion right out of Gone With the Wind complete with four roman columns that stood guard on either side of an entryway large enough to shove a grand piano through. The twin doors leading to the interior of the massive structure— that towered some thirty feet over my head—were massive constructs made of what appeared to be heavy gage steel. From my days in the army I recognized the windows were the type designed to stop every type of munitions short of a howitzer, and even that would have to be fired at close range. The house was a fortress.

And the surrounding grounds were bursting with colorful flower beds with red, purple, yellow, and pink. Chrysanthemum's, begonia, black-eyed Susan's and Jacob's ladder were everywhere. Someone had a green thumb. Given the bucks these people had they likely had a gardener or two or three on the payroll.

The twin doors swung open as the car came to a stop and the black Mr. Clean hopped out—he moved faster than I would have thought him capable given his mass—and held the passenger door open. Ms. Robespierre stepped out with the chauffeur holding one of her hands in his meaty paw. I shuffled across the long leather bench seat and stepped out. The chauffer— who's name was Butch—didn't offer me his hand in fact he glared at me.

"Love you too," I whispered just loud enough for the behemoth to hear me. I could see the burst of anger in his eyes and the muscles of his massive arms rippled beneath his suit as he restrained himself from tearing me in half like he no doubt did to the Yellow Pages. This visit with the rich and infamous had the potential to be a lot of fun.

I followed Ms. Robespierre to the door where a real tuxedoed butler stood beside the entry way. Of course, he looked more like a mob enforcer in a monkey suit than an English butler. He was the white version of Butch the bodyguard. I wondered if he made more on this gig than as a WWE wrestler. He certainly had the build for that line of work. Difference was the average WWE wrestler didn't have the bulge of a cannon in a shoulder holster beneath his suit jacket.

What was it with these people? Had a war broken out I hadn't heard about?

"Thank you, Hugo," said Ms. Robespierre, with a slight nod of her head as we entered and the butler closed and bolted the steel doors with the clang of steel on steel. Oh goody, Fortress Robespierre.

"Follow me to the library," ordered Ms. Robespierre. I followed her dutifully with a shrug. If I hadn't I was pretty sure I would have quickly become lost.

A Day Without Sunshine

There were four sets of heavy twin oak doors that led off the foyer and a massive spiral staircase that led to the upper floors. The floor was grey and white speckled marble and there was a large crystal chandelier that hung from the ceiling, which was at least twenty feet high. Man, I'd hate to have to pay the heat and light bills for this castle.

Ms. Robespierre chose what was behind twin doors number four to our left. We entered a room lined with oak shelves that ran from waist high to the ceiling and covered every wall.

A woman, with an angry jagged scar across her left cheek, dressed in a white maid's uniform, poured what smelled like orange pekoe tea into fine white china cups from a solid silver tea pot set on a silver tray that rested on a round solid oak table. The table was book ended by matching burgundy leather Canterbury wing chairs. Next to each chair was floor a lamp. The cone-shaped hood directed the light from the bulb onto the person seated in the chair. Imagine, a library were someone actually read a book? What will they think of next?

Ms. Robespierre indicated, with a sweep of her left hand, I should sit. Like the good little PI I am I sat.

The maid, with one blue and one green eye, dirty brown hair, a pale complexion, and a slight paunch around her middle appeared to be in her mid-forties, handed me one the cups of tea on a saucer. I nodded and smiled thinly at her but her expression was blank as if she didn't see me. She turned and did likewise to Ms. Robespierre then left the room closing the door behind her with a soft thud.

"How well did you know Sunshine, Mr. Stiletto?" said Ms. Robespierre before she took a tentative nip at the hot tea.

"Your sister's name is Sunshine?" I said.

"I take it you didn't know her then?"

I shook my head and took a sip of the tea. I felt the hot bitter liquid burn as it hit my taste buds then traveled down my throat.

A door hidden behind a wall of books opened and a man dressed in a black sweatshirt, black jean, and black Nike's appeared. He had wiry dirty blonde hair cut into a flat top and piercing blue eyes. His face was hairless, smooth and tanned. Given his medium build and wiry physique I suspected he jogged. In my world we call joggers people who run for their lives, in this world that's how they stay in shape. It was hard to imagine running for fun in my world of unpaid bookies and assorted street toughs.

A Day Without Sunshine

"I'll make him talk, Penny!" The unidentified man lunged across the room at me. With the flick of my wrist I splashed hot tea across his square jawed mug. He howled, his hands covered his face and he stumbled backward until he fell against a wall of books.

"Was that really necessary?" said Ms. Robespierre dryly. "Nathan only wanted to talk."

"When a man comes at me with blood in his eye I usually react poorly, self preservation being what it is," I said, with a faint smile on my lips. "May I call you Penny?"

Nathan had slid to the carpeted floor whimpering like a wounded puppy his hands still held over his reddened features.

Penny Robespierre ignored my suggestion of familiarity. "I'd like to introduce you to Nathan Barber, my fiancé. Please excuse his rash behavior; he tends to be wound a little too tight for his own good."

I smiled. "Well now, that's very different. When's the happy day?"

"It was to be this Saturday but now I'm not so sure." Her gaze drifted over her fiancée like she was examining the on-sale ground chuck at the supermarket. "Now that's Sunshine's dead I'm not sure there's any need at all."

"But darling," said a suddenly alert Nathan, who'd risen to his feet and made his way to stand beside his betrothed's right side. "I love you and I want to be married—"

"To my money," Penny Robespierre finished for him sarcastically.

Nathan was either an Academy Award winning actor, or the most persuasive liar on the planet, evidenced by the look of abject horror on his second degree burned face. He certainly made me a believer.

"I'm afraid I don't understand…" I said.

Penny Robespierre turned slightly in her chair, the polished leather squeaked softly, and I detected the scent of her cinnamon tinged perfume over the odor of her over heated fiancé.

"When our father died seven years ago he made a stipulation in his will that if the two of us survived the first one to marry would inherit the bulk of his estate…."

"And the other?"

Penny shrugged and suddenly avoided eye contact, the powerful woman once more a little girl. "She would get a trust of two million dollars with which to live a comfortable life, wanting for nothing, and the use of the guest house on the property."

"So I gather the estate is large…"

A Day Without Sunshine

"Forty-seven billion."

"Huh, uhhh…I see…" Of course what I saw was a clear motive for murder. Now I knew why she wanted to hire a low rent dick like yours truly. And it explained Fort Apache. But…

"What if one of you died…prematurely or, to be blunt, what if one of you had an unexplained accident?"

"If one of us aided in the demise of the other then the will would be null and void and the survivor would get nothing." She looked up into my eyes and hers narrowed. "I don't know about you, Mr. Stiletto, but once you've had the taste of a jewel encrusted spoon you're unwilling to settle for stainless steel."

"Yes, I can see that," I said. Since my cutlery was usually of the plastic take out variety stainless steel was a luxury item to me.

"Well, then I gather you want me to find out who killed your sister…the question is why?"

Her perfectly plucked eyebrows rose in surprise on her baby-bottom smooth forehead. "Haven't you heard of sisterly love, Mr. Stiletto?"

Nathan, who had been silent to this point, snorted loudly.

Penny turned her head sharply and glared at her paramour.

R.G. Crossley

If it were possible I swear his face actually became redder and his eyes dropped to the floor to avoid the bullets that streamed from her eyes at him.

I sighed. I did need the money. I was planning to blow this town soon and why not use rich people's greenbacks to fund my ride? "OK, Ms. Robespierre. I get five hundred a day, plus expenses. I need the first five hundred now--in cash. I also require a list of places your sister might have been in the last forty eight hours, and a list of names, telephone numbers, and addresses of known associates and friends."

I shifted my body weight forward in the chair until my cheeks were near the edge then leaned toward her. "I was wondering…did Sunshine have a fiancée?" My gaze travelled upward to the cowardly Nathan. "Ya know, like 'ol Nate here."

"Not that I know of," Ms. Robespierre said bluntly. "My sister enjoys…enjoyed partying. She had many lovers. I hate to speak ill of the dead but… Sunshine was a slut. What man of quality and breeding would want a harlot and a drunk for a wife?"

"Yes," I agreed with a nod. "What man indeed?" I saw Nathan's robust features pale and his eyes go wide.

***

Half an hour later I was in a cab headed for my office.

A Day Without Sunshine

In my pocket were the five hundred, ten Benjamin's, and the two lists. One had the names of Sunshine Robespierre's usual haunts, the other was a list of names and addresses. It seemed little Sunshine had spread herself pretty thin. The list had fifty names. It would take me a month to track down everyone on the list. I needed help and I knew just who to call. My own personal cavalry, Lyle Crowder, and his sidekick Wally the weasel would be more than happy to shake these folks trees.

At least the list of hangouts was shorter, with five names. Two were nightclubs for the jet set crowd, while three were twenty-four hour restaurants, two of which were on the wrong side of the tracks. These names I planned to keep to myself—at least for now.

Before I went to my office, and called Crowder, I wanted to freshen up first. I'd shower at the bar and put on a fresh shirt. I looked at my Timex. Mrs. Spitz should have returned my dry-cleaning to Mickey's bar by now. Mickey cut me a lot of slack given I was his best customer, and the fact that we had become friends.

As the cab turned onto my street I saw the flashing lights of an ambulance and several police cars. When we came to a stop outside Mickey's I spotted Crowder's unmarked forest green Chevy.

At the front entrance to the bar, the wood framed glass door was propped open, were two uniforms one male, one female. I paid the driver and walked toward to the female cop my eyes avoiding the male cop.

Her cool blue eyes watched me intently as I approached.

"Hello," I said as a small danced over my lips. "Is Detective Crowder around?"

"And who are you?" she said her voice deep and sexy.

"Stiletto. Jazz Stiletto."

Her eyes smiled. She nodded her head to indicate Lyle was inside Mickey's.

I reached inside to the inner pocket of my suit jacket and pulled out my wallet.

"You gonna bribe me?" she asked with an amused glance at her partner who smirked.

I handed her a business card from my wallet. Every time I arrive in a new city the first thing I do is get business cards.

I gave the female cop a wide toothy smile. "Of course not, officer. That would be illegal. No, I'd like you to take my card to Detective Crowder and tell him I'm out here. I'm certain he'd like to speak with me."

The female cop whose name tag read L Ribowitz frowned as she eyes scanned my card.

"Phil, you stay here and keep an eye on this guy. I'll get the detective." Phil nodded his hands at his sides as if he were waiting for me to draw. Guy had seen too many westerns.

Two minutes later Lyle appeared with Wally in tow. He walked right up to me grabbed my left shoulder, spun me around, and pushed me hard into the wall next to the door. He then grabbed my left arm and bent it behind me. I felt the cold steel of handcuff being locked on my wrist. Next, with his full weight pressing me hard into the wall, he grabbed my other arm and snapped the cuff on my right wrist after twisting it behind my back. He gripped the collar of my suit jacket and pulled me backward. I felt the trickle of blood from one nostril and the taste of blood on my lower lip. I was stunned, helpless, and a prisoner.

"Jason Stiletto, I'm arresting you for the murders of Mickey Risk, Agnes Spitz, Sunshine Robespierre, and Bobbi Diamond. You have the right to--"

I didn't hear the rest of his legalese spiel; I knew it by rote anyway. My mind was spinning. How had this happened? I couldn't believe it; first Bobbi and Sunshine, now Mickey and Mrs. Spitz?

"Lyle! What the hell're you doin'? It's me...Jazz!"

Lyle finished reading me my rights and asked me if I understood them, particularly the part about keeping silent.

Wally eyed me evilly. The son of a bitch was enjoying this. I lunged at him and like the coward he was, he took a step backward and stumbled off the curb. The two uniforms exchanged knowing looks and shook their heads.

Lyle snorted in disgust and grabbed my left arm roughly and shoved me against his car. I felt like I'd been run into a brick wall. Black spots danced before my eyes. The cigarette smell coming from my former friend was stronger now that I was in his space.

He flung the passenger door of his unmarked car open, grabbed me again by my jacket collar, threw me bodily into the back seat and slammed the car door behind me.

I heard Lyle's muffled shout to Wally to get behind the wheel and drive. He was going to ride in the back with the prisoner—it took a moment for the fog that in my brain to clear before it registered Lyle meant me.

Lyle climbed in beside me and shoved me hard against the door handle, it dug hard into my side. I winced from the shot of pain that ran up my right side. "Do you have to be so rough?" I grumbled as I straighten to sit upright.

Lyle said nothing, he kept his eyes focused forward his expression hard as granite.

"Where're we going?"

"The station."

I felt the car lurch beneath me and we began to move. The traffic was light and Wally quickly made his way to First and Albright. He stopped at a red light. I decided to try Lyle again.

"Lyle. I don't get it....why do you think I killed those people?"

His head turned slightly this time and one eye looked at me. His lips moved but no words came out. But that didn't matter. I knew what he'd wanted to say. He had just confirmed who was behind the murders. Lyle Crowder, my one remaining friend in the world, knew I was innocent.

When we arrived at the station Wally pulled into a parking spot far from the main entrance. The street lamp over this part of the lot had burned out so it was dark, and since the sky had decided to open up, rain peppered the Chevy's roof with a sound reminiscent of machine gun bullets. Boy, had my hitch in the army ever screwed up my imagination.

"Get lost, Wally." Esper opened the driver's door and quickly disappeared into the gloom.

Once we were alone with the rain and the stale air of cigarettes Lyle turned to look grim faced at me. The look behind his pained eyes told me the case of Sunshine Robespierre was at an end, or I was at an end. I also knew I had to fix this mess. Someone had to pay…for Mickey, for Mrs. Spitz…even for Sunshine. They had made this personal. Even if it meant my life I had to avenge them.

"I have to leave town," I said flatly.

Lyle nodded. "You OK? Sorry I was so rough. Had to make it look good. You gotta piece?"

I did. It was a Walther PPK, the James Bond gun. I kept it in an ankle holster. Won it in a poker game a few years back. I doubt the gangster I won it from bothered to register it, I know I certainly hadn't.

Funny thing was Lyle hadn't searched me when he arrested me. Since that's standard police procedure it meant who ever had been watching didn't know police procedure. I replayed the image of the street outside Mickey's bar in mind. Yes. The white limo had been there. "Nope. Sorry, I don't carry."

Lyle looked disappointed. He shrugged and reached behind his suit jacket to the small of his back and pulled out a Smith and Wesson nine millimetre automatic. It was his back up piece.

A Day Without Sunshine

All cops carry a back up in case they get into a less than clean shoot or they need extra firepower. He handed me the gun. "Use this to hit me across the face." Lyle reached behind me and undid the handcuffs.

"I can't —"

"Do it or we're both dead." I nodded. I knew he was right. "I'll create a new name for you but you have to get out of town tonight. It has to look like you escaped."

"Why?"

"I have a family, Jazz…my son needs a father. But I also have a conscience. If you went to prison you'd have a shiv in you within the first week. You got too close, too fast. You were taken to the house to scope out how smart you were. Between us the frame job they tried at first didn't work so more murders with a hot tip to the chief's office did the trick. The chief and the DA both have expensive tastes."

"Money and power?"

"Forty-Seven billion buys a lot insurance."

I nodded and studied the gun. I ran my index finger up the barrel and felt the roughness where the serial number had been filed off. Suddenly I lashed out and caught Lyle hard across the head. I heard a crack of bone and his outline fell forward onto the seat in from of me. I smelled blood.

In the darkness I could hear him breathing.

Good. Now I had some unfinished business. Then would I leave town.

***

I placed Lyle's unconscious form against a chain link fence at the rear of the parking lot then drove away slowly so as not to arouse any suspicion.

I arrived at the chateau Robespierre just as the long white limousine pulled up to the front doors.

I watched as the hulking bodyguard opened the passenger door nearest the front doors. The butler stood with a silver tray upon which rested a single champagne glass. A victory drink no doubt.

I moved into position for a shot. The one thing they did well in the army was teach you how to shoot people. And I'd been good at it.

Now when you're going to kill someone, in fact three someone's you have to do it quickly. Unlike Hollywood where killers have these long expositions about the reasons and make the hero sweat it out before they do them, the reality is it takes about three seconds per shot. In a total of nine seconds I'd drilled three perfectly round holes dead centre into three foreheads.

The bullets ripped apart whatever intelligence these people had. They were no more.

***

A Day Without Sunshine

I picked up my new identification papers from locker number seven at the bus station the next morning. I'd shaved and with five hundred dollars I'd bought a pair of blue jeans and a checkered work shirt and tanned work boots. I also had a duffle bag with an extra set of matching clothes and three pairs of underwear , socks and a shaving kit. The remainder of the money, three hundred and forty-seven dollars and twelve cents, paid for a bus ticket.

The two uniformed cops on the departure platform eyed me over closely. They checked my new driver's license, with the name Allan Harper, then let me board the Greyhound to my future.

The sky was overcast as the bus pulled away and joined traffic headed for the interstate. It started to rain by the time we merged with the traffic headed west.

An older man with steel gray hair who smelled of whiskey sat next to me. He offered me his flask which I gladly accepted. I took a swig, the burning whisky felt good, then handed the silver flask back to him.

In his gruff voice he said, "Looks like another day without sunshine."

"Yeah," I agreed, "another day without sunshine."

R.G. Crossley

Dangerous Waters

I SHIVERED. NOT BECAUSE I just left the rain drenched, windswept Tradewinds Casino parking lot. And not because I suffered from the DT's, and really needed that first scotch Art the bartender had waiting for me in the Pacific Coast Bar on the second floor of the casino. It was because I almost tripped over the bloody corpse of Lincoln City's favorite used book dealer, Simon Yardley.

Simon lay at my feet in a puddle of water and blood, his throat marred by a nasty slash.

Simon's chocolate brown knit pants, and pale green shirt, were soaked through with water — salt water if my olfactory senses were still accurate.

"Freeze!" I froze, my heart racing.

I heard the familiar sound of a hammer being cocked on a revolver.

Back in the day I'd witnessed a lot of thirty-eight specials being fired at paper targets. And I knew all too well the damage hot lead could do to human flesh. Unfortunately, I also knew the casino security guards were older than dirt.

Old age, poor reflexes, and clouded minds, when paired with deadly force. It made me nervous.

As a writer I pride myself on knowing a lot of otherwise useless information. In this case I know too much.

"Hey, pops." I spoke slowly, and I hoped friendly, as I raised my hands over my head. "It's me Bert Sump." I glanced over my left shoulder and saw Parker Thomas, his gun gripped in both trembling hands. His gray-blue eyes flitted between me and poor Simon.

I closed my eyes and sighed.

Park is a fan. Since my fame from the best seller days left the building with Elvis, having one loyal fan is a treasure more valuable than gold.

"I know, Mr. Simp, but don't move. The sheriff is on his way."

"Huh, Park, can I at least lower my arms?"

"Yeah, sure, Mr. Simp." With relief I let my arms drop to my sides. Physical exertion and I are old adversary's.

At three in the a.m., the sheriff, a new man I'd not met, was no doubt at home sawing down forests. Besides a December storm was in full swing outside. On a day like this a warm bed is man's best friend.

Winter storms and high winds make the ocean go mad at this time of year. Impassionate television news anchors, with perfect teeth and sculpted hair, love to tell tales of fierce waves pounding the shores of Lincoln City threatening to drag the summer-settlers way-too-expensive homes into the sea.

Local radio told of the powerful surf overpowering the breakwater at the Green Creek Bridge to sweep away a large section of highway. This cut Lincoln City in two.

I was grateful to be on the casino side of the highway, so I was nearer Art's bar.

And, according to the radio, the torrent coming from the boiling, ink-black clouds had washed out the highways both in and out of town. I considered trying to figure out how large a cubit is, but since I am a sinner by nature I decided against it. God doesn't want such as me in His heaven.

A distinctly feminine voice behind me startled me, "Hey, Parker." A draw of breath then she added, "Whoa, is that a dead body?"

"Hi, Deputy. Yes, and this is the killer."

Great, a woman deputy who thinks dead bodies are cool, and an old man who thinks I killed a book dealer. What possible motive could I have to murder Simon; he refuses to carry my third stink book because it's only good for lining the bottom of bird cages?

Of course, when I thought about it that's really not a bad motive.

"Deputy, do you mind if I stop being the model for the ice sculpture on the buffet so we can talk?"

"Sure."

I turned and met the pretty brunette's big brown eyes. She filled out her tan-colored sheriff department uniform like Pam Anderson filled out her bathing suit. Without thinking I blurted, "Hey, beautiful where you been all my life?"

The corners of her wide mouth curled slightly. "You're kidding, right?"

My cheeks grew warm. "Yeah, of course."

Her tanned brow wrinkled and one eyebrow arched. "Aren't you Max Acton?"

While I'm always pleased to be recognized but that name still makes me cringe. I made a mental note to send my former agent another hate e-mail for insisting on the inane pseudonym.

"My real name is Bert Simp."

The deputy crossed her arms over the swell of her bosom. "Hmmm, I think I like the fake name better."

Great, she thinks Max Acton is the better name. I suppressed the urge to groan. "Have we met?"

"Nope." Her eyes shifted to scan the dead body. "Isn't that Simon Yardley?"

"Yes," said Park who, much to my relief, had holstered his gun. "I think he's been murdered."

The deputy's eyes met mine and a brief smile passed over her lips. I shrugged. "Deputy Marne Locke." Her eyes stayed locked on mine while she tilted her head to indicate Simon. "You know him?"

"Certainly, he's a friend."

Marne nodded then her gaze shifted to Park. "What about you, Parker?"

Park shrugged his narrow shoulders while shifting his feet uneasily. His leather holster squeezed in time to his movements. New leather does tend to be noisy.

"How do you know Yardley?" I walked across the casino floor to liberate a chair from the row of chairs near the entrance doors. The chairs were padded and my butt was getting cold. It was like there was a draft coming from somewhere. Very odd for a casino to have drafts.

They like to make the guests—a very genteel term for sheep ripe for the fleecing—as comfortable as possible, at least until they've emptied their bank accounts into the slot machines, or added to the bankers stacks of chips at the craps table.

The lights flickered then dimmed. I looked up at the lights on the ceiling far above the casino floor. What's going on?

Marne must be a mind reader because she cleared up the mystery immediately. "I was upstairs in the office when I got the call."

"About Simon?"

"Ho, not that. The roads are washed out. The Sheriff is madder 'en a wet dog with fleas that he can't get here." She paused and crinkles appeared at the corners of her eyes telling me she didn't much care for the new sheriff. "No, I was already here meeting with the Casino's Chairman of the Board about a theft."

The lights flickered again. I thought they were going to go out all together. After a few seconds of uncertainty they steadied but the shadows in the far corners deepened. I hope they paid their light bill this month.

"What's going on?" I walked to the back of switches next to entrance to the men's room and used my index finger to flick one to the off position.

A pot light directly over head went dark so I flicked the switch to the on position but the pot light didn't come back on. This can't be good.

Marne grunted. "That's what I thought."

"What?" Park's voice was tinged with fear.

Marne explained. "The storm knocked out the main transformer for the casino. The backup generators are beginning to have cascading failures."

She walked to the bottom of the stairs leading to the second floor. One hand rested on the polished brass rail running up both sides of the spiral staircase, the other had rested on the butt of her nine millimetre Glock.

"I suggest we locate the chairman and hopefully he has a place we can hole up until the storm passes. We don't have much time before the casino goes dark."

I frowned. Some things she said made my alarm bells go off. Maybe it was the thriller writer in me, but I knew she was lying or, if not lying, she'd omitted a fact or two.

"Ummm, deputy, I have a couple of questions." Both eyebrows on Marne's forehead rose. Maybe I'm wrong but my sixth sense screamed at me I was about to enter dangerous waters.

She stared at me with one booted foot on the bottom step.

"If Simon's been murdered, and the roads are washed out, then it means the killer's still in the casino. And why would the chairman still be in his office at this hour?"

She moved her foot off the top step and turned to face me. Her fingers played with the butt of her pistol. Her brow wrinkled and her eyes were uncertain. It was as if she was wrestling with a decision.

She was making me nervous.

I ran my tongue over my dry lips and thought about that scotch waiting for me. Maybe I'd ask Art to make it a double.

A gunshot echoed from above punctuating the silence. It was then I realized the slot machines were silent, and the only people here were me, Park and Marne. I dove to the side of the staircase hoping to use it as a shield. I glanced at Park in time to see him collapse to his knees. His fingers covered a growing red blotch in the center of his chest and his eyes were wide with surprise.

A pitiful moan escaped his lips just as his eyes rolled up in his head. He fell forward to land face down on the carpet with a muffled thud. Like Simon, Park was stone cold dead.

Marne snorted. "Great. Why did he have to kill Parker?"

She shook her head then disappeared up the stairs.

I was alone.

I'm a writer. The nature of my work makes me a solitary creature who only leaves his cave for food and water and, in my case, for visits with his friendly neighborhood bartender. Unfortunately, I don't think Art is serving this morning. Besides I may have had my last drink. I'd never felt as alone as I did right now.

Banks of lights winked out plunging most of the casino into darkness. Eerie shadows created by the remaining lights covered the walls, the slot machines and gaming tables. From where I lay on my belly next to the staircase I could see bolts of lightening flash across the ink black sky through the glass entrance doors .

I considered making a break for the entrance. I could sit in my car and lock the doors. But since I was one of only a few cars in the parking lot I'd be easy to find. Not a good idea. I shivered.

I froze when I heard voices drift from somewhere over my head. One had to be Marne's, but the other two were definitely male, and I definitely couldn't identify them.

I closed my eyes and willed my rapidly beating heart to slow. I had to clear my mind in order to think rationally.

If this was a book, and I was the hero, how would I get out of this situation?

Think, dummy, think.

What were they after? No one just kills someone without a reason. Robbery, hate, love, rivalry, anger, for fun…these are all possible motives for murder. Unfortunately, sometimes there was no reason at all. Sometimes the killer explained it was just because they could, like the reason crazies climb mountains.

But in this case it had to be for a reason. Didn't Marne say something about a theft? And last week Simon told me he'd bought a rare and valuable manuscript at an estate sale. He said he was going to make some real coin, and finally be able to retire.

I shook my head. Simon probably told everyone who came into his store about the manuscript. He probably even showed it to a few people.

And Marne seemed to know it was Simon dead on the floor. Like she knows the name of a seventy-plus–year-old used book dealer? Yeah, sure a young, beautiful cop travels in the same social circles as a grey-haired book dealer? I don't think so.

I rose to my knees, then to a crouch, keeping my body as low as possible beside the staircase. Glancing over my shoulder I spotted a door marked EMPLOYEES ONLY.

It's amazing what you don't see unless you have to. I'd never noticed that door before even though it was next to the entrance to the men's room. It proves the urge to empty my bloated bladder is stronger than my observation skills. I made mental note of that fact. I could use it my next novel, if I ever write it that is. The sad fact is I haven't sold a book in two years. My bank account is nearly as exhausted as I am.

I kept a low profile as I ran to the door and stepped through into a dimly lit hallway. The battery powered emergency lights in the hallway cut the gloom, but there were still areas shrouded in darkness. I shivered. A bullet could end this escape at any moment. I paused and held my breath. Nothing happened. I'm good so far.

The hallway had two branches, one going to the left, the other to the right.

I mentally flipped a coin and went left. I wasn't sure what I was going to do, or where I was going, all I knew for sure is anywhere but the casino floor—or the parking lot—had to be safer than a room with two dead bodies.

As I walked I thought about Marne. The deputy knew me as well as Simon, but she knew me as my pseudonym, not my real name.

I considered this and, since my books were out of print, the only conclusion had to be that she had been to Simon's store and seen my first book on the display stand on the counter. My picture was on the jacket so she must have picked it up to look at it.

I was a lot younger in the picture, but I couldn't help but be flattered. A swollen ego is truly a terrible thing.

At the end of the hall I was met with another door. I tried the brass handle and found it unlocked. Good.

I opened the door to find stairs leading up into darkness. I considered going back to where I started but decided to press on.

Looking around I found a door stop in the shadows. I opened the door and shoved the door stop under the bottom to keep it open. What little light there was in the hallway would help me see the steps.

My stomach tightened as fear coursed through me. I took in a few deep breaths to steady my nerves and to stop my hands from shaking.

I'm a thriller writer, damn it. I write about serial killers and blood and death all the time. I had to get a grip or I'd never get out of this alive.

I opened my eyes and blew out a shaky breath then started up the stairs.

The odor of lemons and garlic became stronger and stronger as I made my up the stairs. Finally I reached the last step and stopped and strained to listen for any sound. My heart beat rapidly in my ears.

I yelled as suddenly a bright light forced me to shut my eyes.

"Hey, Bert," said a very familiar voice. "Want the usual?"

Art. Art's involved? I licked my lips as the image of a glass of amber scotch filled my mind. "As a matter of fact, yes Art that would be welcome about now." I raised my hands to shield my eyes from the light. "Do you have to shine that light in my eyes?"

Art chuckled and the light dropped to the floor. I blinked to clear my sight and saw the vague outline of Marne, her hands on her hips, and Art holding a flashlight and a gun. The gun he pointed at me.

"You picked the wrong night to need a drink," Art said his voice bitter and harsh in my ears. My friendly neighborhood bartender was suddenly not so friendly.

"Listen, Art, whatever's going on here is none of my business. I don't know where the manuscript is —"

Stupid is as stupid does. Me and my big yap.

"Oh. So you know about the manuscript." Art glanced at Marne. "We should kill him," he said dispassionately.

"No. Not yet. He wouldn't like it." She paused and I worried she might change her mind. The next few seconds could be my last. Finally she added, "Let's take him to the chairman."

Art seemed disappointed to lower the barrel of the automatic. I had no idea he was so vicious. Sure he's a veteran, and had been in combat, but Iraq is a world away from the genteel streets of Lincoln City. I decided then to get a new bartender.

Art grins at me as he uses the gun like a pointer waving me to his left and then toward a door marked by the circle of white light from the flashlight. I stopped at the door and waited.

"Open it," said Marne.

I did and was surprised to find the office inside fully lit. The gun barrel poked my back to urge me forward so I stepped inside.

We were greeted with a grunt by a large man with puffy, ruddy cheeks, and dark sunglasses over his eyes sat behind a smoked glass desk. Covering his bulk was an expensive looking navy suit, with a dark blue shirt and maroon tie. His breathing was heavy and the odor of lemon and garlic was stronger than ever in here.

I winced when Art prodded me harder with the gun and I took a seat across the desk from the man who I assumed was the chairman.

Marne moved to stand by a potted palm tree in a corner of the office. Art went to stand next to the desk his hazel eyes watching me, the gun hanging at his right side, the barrel pointed at the floor.

"Mr. Acton?" said the large man his voice husky and thick. I nodded. What's the use it fighting it. The corners of the man's mouth turned up slightly. "My name is Barbas. I'm the chairman." He eased back in the leather executive chair and folded his sausage sized fingers in his lap. "I'm a fan of your books," he explained, "which is why you're still alive." Another fan? I guess I'm more famous that I thought.

Barbas removed his sunglasses revealing one blue and one green eye. I'd just entered a James Bond movie.

He leaned closer to me and his strange eyes narrowed. "Tell me what you know about the manuscript."

He didn't say it but I hoped he meant if I told him he might let me live. These folks are obviously eliminating any possible connections to themselves.

"Uhhh, Well..." I struggled for the right words. Of course, being as nervous as virgin bride on her wedding night certainly didn't help. "Simon told me he had the manuscript, and that he bought it at an estate sale."

"Did he show it to you?" His brow wrinkled and I knew my next words would seal my fate.

I mentally flipped my last coin then shook my head. "No. I have no idea what the manuscript is, or who wrote it."

Barbas eased back in his chair and smiled. He glanced at Marne. "Good, he knows nothing. But he's seen us. Take him downstairs and dispose of him like the others."

My coin toss had come up dead.

Marne shrugged. "Ok, Mr. Chairman."

She uncrossed her arms and walked to stand over me. "Let's go."

I stood and, without looking back, we walked out the door. Marne closed it behind us leaving Art and the Chairman behind. Good riddance to bad news. It looked like good riddance to everything.

As we reached the top of the spiral staircase I muttered, "Dangerous waters."

"What?" said Marne.

"Outside," I indicated the entrance doors below us. Dawn was nearing and in the first light of day I could make out the angry whitecaps of giant waves pounding the shore in the distance. I glanced at Marne walking to my right, a step behind me, and realized her attention was on the doors. Now was my chance.

Pulling up before I took another step I stuck my foot out and Marne tripped over it. Her momentum carried her forward. Off balance, unable to control her fall, she rolled down the stairs with a cry of pain that abruptly ended when she landed in a heap at the bottom.

I raced down the stairs and dropped to my haunches then released her Glock from its holster. The gun was surprisingly heavy in my hand.

I heard an angry voice from above and without thinking pointed the gun into the darkness and fired. The muzzle flash blinded me for a few seconds, but I heard a cry of pain followed by a thump which meant I'd hit the target.

I looked down at Marne and realized her neck was broken. Her eyes were open and her arms and legs were at unnatural angles.

The thud of heavy footsteps receding into the distance above my head meant the big man was heading for the hills. Let him go. Where is he going to run to in the middle of a winter storm in Lincoln City?

I decided to call it a day. Four bodies was enough for one day.

Dangerous Waters

I raised my drink and made a toast to the dead. Thanks for the rotten memories. I downed the drink in one swallow then steeled myself to for the long march home in the driving rain and fierce winds outside these walls.

Dangerous waters breed dangerous times. At least it certainly did for four of my fellow humans.

About the Author

Russ Crossley writes romance under the name R.G. Hart, mystery/suspense under the name R.G. Crossley, and science fiction and fantasy under his own. This year there will be re-issues the romantic comedies, Bachelorette: Zombie Edition by Champagne Books, and Antique Virgin by 53rd Street Publishing, paranormal romantic comedy, Zomopolis, and a new western romance entitled, The Fire In Their Hearts co-authored with R.S. Meger. In addition the near future suspense novel, The Last Serial Killer by R.G. Crossley will be released soon.

He has sold several short stories that have appeared in anthologies from Pocket Books, St. Matins Press, at Smashwords, Amazon, and other e-retail sites.

With his wife, romance author R.S. Meger, he owns and operates a small press publishing company, 53rd Street Publishing. The company began in April 2011 and now has over one hundred e-book titles and two print titles, with more planned in 2012.

He is a member of SF Canada and the Greater Vancouver Chapter of Romance Writers of America. He is also an alumni of the Oregon Coast Professional Fiction Writers Master Class taught by award winning author/editors, Kristine Katherine Rusch and Dean Wesley Smith.

To find a complete listing of his work check out his website http://www.rghart.com, http://russstory. blogspot.com.Razor's blog can be found at http://razorandedge.blogspot.com

Other books by the Author

Titles as R.G. Crossley

Short Stories

Razor and Edge Mysteries
The Kidnapping of Billy Buttons
String of Pearls
Death by Clown
Beggin' For Murder
Ragged Ice
The Grand Central Mystery

Non-Series Mysteries
A Day Without Sunshine
Mirror Image
Dangerous Waters
Cape Disappointment
Boomerang
The Watcher of Wayburn Street
The Apprentice
Drip!
A Beautiful Friendship and
The Parrot of Doom
Robine's Diary
The Christmas Club
Loose Ends
Skullduggery
Splatter Pattern
It Takes Two

Anthologies
The Adventures of Razor and Edge:
Five Tales From The Quirky Detective Team

Novels
A Bad Case of Loyalty
The Last Serial Killer
Shear Murder

Titles as Russ Crossley

Novels
Attack of the Lushites

Short Stories
Countdown
Shoeless Moe
Round Up At The Burger Bar:
The Story of Trixie Pug,
Parts 1, 2, 3, 4, 5,6,7
Five Minutes
Blossom Queen, Barbarian
The Secret
The Family Line
End of the Flies
With Death You Get the Eggroll
The Penguin Sleeps With The Fishes
Only The Worthy
Hero For A Day
End of Empire
Strange Bedfellows

Big Business
A Perfect Crime
The Wise Guy and The Pirates
In Search of the Perfect Cup
T.I.N. Men
The Legend of G and the Dragonettes
The Incredible Mr. Fix-It
Lock Stock and Barrel
Divided Loyalties
Cave of Wonders
A Family Empire
Until We Meet Again
Dragon Rising

Presents Anthology Series
Five Tales of Urban Fantasy
Five Tales of Bizarre Detectives
Five Tales of Mystery and Suspense
Five Tales of Weird Fantasy
Spies, Detectives, & Heroes
Tales of Twisted Crime
Five Tales of The Unexpected
Tales From Space
10 by Russ Crossley
Round Up At The Burger Bar:
The Story of Trixie Pug, Parts 1- 5
The Beginning
Worlds of Science Fiction and Fantasy
More Tales of Mystery and Suspense
Ladies of the Jolly Roger
Justice Served

Titles as R.G. Hart

Short Stories
Tikka's Big Day
"My Partner the Zombie" —
Hungry For Your Love Anthology
(St. Martin's Press)
Big Hairy Deal
One Red Shoe
A Bad Day in Lunden Texas
Hook Island
Grind Manor

Novels
Bachelorette: Zombie Edition
(Champagne Books)
Antique Virgin
The Fire In Their Hearts
with R.S. Meger (coming soon from Champagne
Books)
Zomopolis